JUDGE
NOT

JUDGE NOT

GEORGE C. VLACHOS

ReadersMagnet, LLC

Judge Not
Copyright © 2024 by George C. Vlachos

Published in the United States of America

Library of Congress Control Number: 2024921702
ISBN   Paperback: 979-8-89091-652-5
ISBN   eBook: 979-8-89091-653-2

All rights reserved. No part of this publication may be reproduced, stored in a retrieval system or transmitted in any way by any means, electronic, mechanical, photocopy, recording or otherwise without the prior permission of the author except as provided by USA copyright law.

The opinions expressed by the author are not necessarily those of ReadersMagnet, LLC.

ReadersMagnet, LLC
10620 Treena Street, Suite 230 | San Diego, California, 92131 USA
1.619. 354. 2643 | www.readersmagnet.com

Book design copyright © 2024 by ReadersMagnet, LLC. All rights reserved.

Cover design by Kent Gabutin
Interior design by Dorothy Lee

CHAPTER 1

Today was an anniversary. It had been a long time since it had been *the* anniversary. She thought about it less and less as time went on. She guessed that that was normal. Her therapist confirmed that notion on many occasions. Regardless, it still popped up once in a while. Here it was again.

Maybe it was the briskness in the October air. Maybe it was the way the autumn sun bounced off the city streets. Maybe it was just that the car service was running late. Something brought her thoughts to that place.

It was the beginning of sixth grade. The excitement of the new school year had barely faded away. She had enjoyed school before that day; she had quite a different outlook about almost everything after that day.

The bus stopped, as it always had, only a few houses from her home. After a quick 'see you later' to her friends at the bus stop she ran home as fast as she could, holding her books with both arms against her chest.

Abigale's (family and friends called her Abby) home was in a quiet neighborhood. The suburban housing development consisted of a circular road with one road coming off it leading to a cul-de-sac and another leading in and out.

Abby's house was a small three-bedroom one at the top of the hill that began its ascent at the first left upon entering the development. She had her own bedroom and it was decorated just the way she liked it. As was typical in Abby's life, her Mom helped.

Rarely was her mother not home when Abby arrived from school. This was one of those days. Her mom had informed both her daughter and her husband at breakfast of her plans to be home a little later that afternoon. Dinner, however, would be on the table at 6:00 as per usual. Abby's dad was always home for dinner.

"Mom said she was gonna be a little late today, but that she would leave the key under mat. Okay, where is it? Oh, here it is. Great!" Her tone was loud enough for only her to hear.

The key did not enter the lock cleanly and as she struggled with it she noticed for the first time that her dad's car was in the driveway. "Finally," she whispered with relief. She entered her home and closed the door behind her.

"Dad! Dad! Are you home?" The question went unanswered.

"Maybe he shared a ride to work today," she said softly. "Dad, are you home?" Her voice echoed through the house. She decided that he wasn't home and went into the kitchen to fix herself a snack.

She put her backpack on a kitchen chair and made her way to the cookie jar. It was almost always at least half full of homemade oatmeal cookies.

She poured herself a large glass of ice-cold milk and settled in at the kitchen table with it and her 3 oatmeal cookies. The milk and cookies tasted great; they always did.

"Oh, I almost forgot," she said softly, finishing her last little bit of milk. "I need to wash my gym clothes for tomorrow." She reached into her back pack, pulled out her crumpled shorts and tee-shirt and headed toward the basement steps.

Abby knew that her Mom would rather that the washer and dryer be on the main floor, but Abby kinda liked going down into the basement to do the wash. The basement was filled with 'stuff' - all kinds of 'stuff'.

There were old clothes that her mom had in a covered clothes rack. Abby liked to unzip the cover and touch the old dresses and skirts, imagining what it might be like to wear them. There was also an old record player with tons of old records from the sixties. Sometimes she would get lost in the music of Joan Baez, Bob Dylan and lots of other artists from that time.

There were so many things from the 'old days' in the basement that she could spend hours down there and many times did just that.

"Let me check to see if there's anything else that needs to be put in the wash." She ran upstairs to check her hamper. She then scurried down the two flights of stairs with her arms so full of clothes that she could barely see over the top of them.

Emptying her arms into the washer, she readied the machine to do its job. After carefully pressing the necessary buttons she stood back and waited for the washer to start its cycle.

At that moment something made her look over at her father's elaborate miniature train set-up. She thought she heard a humming sound. She stared for a moment at the single light bulb that always stayed lit to provide a 'night light' type service in the typically very dark basement.

It illuminated a stark corner where all that could be seen was the juncture of the two gray concrete walls. Above it and to the right was a small basement window that permitted only a small bit of daylight to irradiate that corner.

She rarely wandered to that side. The large table on which the fictitious train town rested, nearly filled that half of the cellar. The town slept under the tiffany light fixture which was draped idly over the silent trains.

The washing machine still filling itself with water, she decided to walk under the stairway to the far corner where the light bulb gently swung. The single bulb which hung over the washer and dryer and the fading light of the autumn sky peeking through the small basement windows were the only light provided.

Barely able to see under the staircase she stopped suddenly. The humming noise was coming from the transformer. *Why was it on? And the train was off the track at 'dead man's curve'.*

Abby walked around the table to where her father's 'engineer's stool' sat empty. The humming transformer, its red light glowing, was positioned on the table within a short reach of the stool.

She stopped and stood silently for a moment. Then she heard herself scream. It was unlike any sound that she ever heard before.

Her father was lying, motionless, next to his stool. His body was in a semi fetal position; a small puddle of blood on the gray tiled Formica floor, surrounded his head.

"Daddy! What's wrong? Can you get up?" As she shouted her words the tears started to flow. She bent down to shake her dad.

She wanted him to get him up. Then everything would be ok.

"Daddy, please get up! Pleeease, Daddy! Please Daddy, get up!"

Then Abby saw the gun. It was a pistol a small one. It was underneath her Dad. She saw it when she shook him.

"Mommy, mommy, something is wrong with Daddy," she screamed as loud as she could, before she realized that no one else was there. She ran up the stairs and out the front door.

She ran to the house next door. Mrs. Wyard would be home, she thought. She was always home. She was an elderly widow who lived alone. She seemed to have more energy than her age should allow. Abby noticed that when Mrs. Wyard walked her small dog, twice daily, like clockwork.

"Mrs. Wyard, come quick! There's something wrong with my Dad! There's a gun!"

"What? Where's your mother, Abby?"

"She's not home. Please hurry," Abby cried out as she fidgeted on the front porch, barely able to hold back the tears.

"Okay dear," Mrs. Wyard responded as she reached for her sweater that hung on the coat rack just inside the front door.

Abby grabbed Mrs. Wyard's hand but she couldn't get her to walk any faster. Abby wanted to run but she didn't.

"Hurry, Mrs. Wyard! Hurry!"

"All right, Dear. All right, Abby. I'm coming."

Mrs. Wyard had been a very good athlete in her youth. She played college basketball at UCLA in the 1940s. In fact, she was an all American during her junior year.

She always considered herself a bit of a pioneer. Women rarely went to college in her day and fewer still traveled across the country to do so. And of course, women's collegiate athletics were not nearly then what they were to become. She was, however, walking as fast as she could now.

"Is he okay? Is he okay? Mrs. Wyard, please tell me he's okay." Abby started to cry again. "Is my daddy okaaay?" She couldn't control her sobbing now.

"No, honey, I'm afraid your Daddy's not okay. Where's the telephone, dear? I need to call the police."

Mrs. Polk came home from the grocery store to find an ambulance and several police cars parked outside her house. Her little girl was standing on the front lawn with her next door neighbor and a female police officer. Mrs. Wyard's arm was around Abby, who was wrapped in a blanket. She wasn't crying any longer. She felt nothing now.

"What happened here? What's going on," Mrs. Polk said as she knelt down next to her daughter.

Abby turned to her mother and with very little emotion said, "Daddy's dead."

"What," Mrs. Polk said softly as she looked up at Mrs. Wyard, and rose slowly to a standing position. "What happened?"

"It looks like a suicide, Dorothy. I'm so sorry. Abby found him. She has been so strong. You should be very proud of her." Mrs. Wyard looked down at Abby as she finished talking.

Abby's mother knelt down next to her and put both her hands on Abby's shoulders. She looked into her daughter's detached eyes and asked softly, "can you tell me what happened, honey?"

"I came home from school and I went downstairs to do some wash." She paused and looked at the house again. Abby turned back to face her Mom. "And I saw Daddy lying on the floor by the railroad town."

Abby paused and looked again at the house as the police personnel came and went. "Oh Mommy," she cried as she collapsed into her mother's arms, "Daddy's gone."

"I know, honey. It's going to be okay." But as Dorothy Polk said those words she began to cry as well. The two Polk girls cried in each other's arms as Mrs. Wyard, not knowing what else to do, kept her steady gaze on the house.

She shed a tear or two, mostly feeling for Abby. She knew what it was like to lose a husband, but to lose a father at such a young age and suicide! Oh, my, she said to herself, *how horrible for Abby!*

CHAPTER 2

The car, which was to transport Abby to the Judge's Award Dinner, was here. Finally! Abby hated these affairs. She was 'on' all day. Night time was her time. Tonight was a little different though. She was going to be honored; Judge of the year. That's why the car. It was sent for her. *I guess it's a big deal. Oh well, smile and make the best of it.*

Her journey to a judgeship was quicker than most. She had gotten involved in politics out on Long Island, early on, while still in law school. The line 'politics is dirty,' which she supposed was as old as the political system itself, was never truer anywhere else. She learned that very quickly.

She knew of at least one law school friend who never did get it. When she thought of him and his still unsuccessful quest for a judgeship, which wasn't very often, she blamed his failure on either too little sophistication or too much morality.

He was given direction that was misleading at best and he was made promises that were never intended to be fulfilled. It was a scenario that happens more often than not on the Island of Long, especially in Abby's former county.

Abby's road was much different. She was able to secure a cross endorsement from a few minor parties, the most important of which was from the local conservative party. It was a practice that was frowned upon by the feds but nonetheless was typically done and proved to be quite effective in recent years.

It didn't hurt that she was an attractive young lawyer. She wore her silky dark brown hair then as she did now; just below her shoulders. Abby had big soulful brown eyes that were complimented by her high cheek bones and baby smooth skin. When Abby smiled, men melted; another fact that she learned early on.

She made political friends quickly and often, and she did what she needed to do to obtain her position on the New York State Supreme Court Bench. She was not always proud of her actions, but she was proud of where she was. Most days that was enough. *Thank goodness her mom, God rest her soul, would never know.*

Although elected to the Bench in Suffolk County, she had recently requested and been granted a transfer to Brooklyn. She now worked in Brooklyn, lived in Brooklyn and played, mostly in Brooklyn. She loved it; all of it.

Money was rarely an obstacle in Abby's life. She was paid adequately for her Judgeship but that salary alone would not be able to support her lifestyle.

It seems that unbeknownst to anyone, even Abby's mom, her dad was investing in blue-chip stocks dating back to the 50's and had accumulated quite a substantial portfolio at the time of his death.

Abby's mom had put the high seven figure amount in a trust for Abby shortly after her dad had died. Abby's mom lived off the interest of the trust, a small life insurance policy and her job as a clerk for the Suffolk County Labor Department, until she passed away.

Abby didn't touch the principal. There was no need. The interest off the trust, coupled with her Judge's salary was more than sufficient to support her present lifestyle.

Her mom had taught her the meaning of a dollar but, it actually started with her dad. Abby remembered the day he took her to the bank to open a savings account. It was only a month or two before he died. She was so excited.

She loved doing anything with her dad. He was big and strong, but always exhibited a gentle touch with his little girl. She felt safe, secure and most of all loved when she was with him. And he was very funny. He always made her giggle.

"Daddy," she would scream, "Stop teasing me. Let me have the quarter!" when he would hide a coin in his large, mitt-like hands. Sometimes he would use a half dollar, but most times it was a quarter. She could never open his hand to get the coin, but he always gave it to her so she could put it into her piggy bank.

Once the piggy bank was filled, he told her they would roll the coins together and deposit the rolls into her new savings account. But that day when they went to the bank together, he signed some papers and handed the lady at the bank a crisp $100.00 dollar bill to start Abby's account. Abby was so excited. Then her dad took her for ice cream. It seemed that all her memories of her dad were fond ones. The memories were few but lasting. The time with him was so short. Sadly, she thought, those happy memories faded with every passing year. Sometimes it was even hard for her to remember exactly what his large round smiling face looked like.

With that thought, sadness overcame her. She reached for a tissue in her pocketbook and dabbed the corner of her eyes with it. As she returned the tissue to its place, she noticed a mark of some kind on her brand-new black suede pumps.

"What is this now," she said in an aggravated whisper. "These shoes are brand-new." She bent down and used the tissue to successfully wipe away the piece of lint and found a place in her pocketbook to place the tissue until it could be discarded later.

Abby looked up to see that they were arriving at their destination. As she was helped out of the large black car by the driver, she looked at the entrance of the Waldorf, an entrance she had seen many times in the past. Every time, however, she was impressed with its elegant simplicity.

The lobby was chock-full of old-world charm, something of which Abby never grew tired. Her stride through the lobby was one of pride and confidence. She looked great and she knew it.

Her floor-length black gown was as understated as such a dress with rising middle slit could be. Pearls shone brightly from her ears and neck and the dark stockings lead down to those black suede shoes, which finished the beautiful outfit.

Abby could wear most anything and look great. Even now in her mid forties she had the figure of a twenty-five year old. It was an athletic look. She had a v-shaped back that accentuated a small waist. She had always been a bit disappointed in the size of her breasts but she accepted the fact that they seemed to fit her body.

It also helped that she was well aware that she had legs to 'to die for'.

"Good evening Ms. Polk. May I take your wrap?"

"Thank you, my dear. Yes, please. You can take my wrap. Thank you.

The young coat-check girl put down her cell phone just long enough to make her inquiry. "That's a beautiful dress," she continued."

"Congratulations, your Honor."

"Thank you, John," Abby responded as she put her claim ticket in her black clutch.

John Updike was a local attorney who had been in Abby's courtroom many times. She liked him well enough and he was a competent lawyer but he was a bit of kiss-ass. A lot of the lawyers were. In Abby's book, respect taken up a notch was brown-nosing; although sometimes it was hard to distinguish between the two.

In the case of John Updike, it bordered on outright flirting. That's where Abby drew the line. She never socialized with anyone that she associated with on a professional level, except, of course affairs like this one tonight.

She was not seated at her assigned table very long before the waiter took her drink order. *This was a champagne night,* she thought to herself. After all, Judge of the Year honors don't happen every day.

"Abby, Abby Polk is that you?"

Abby looked up, she hesitated "I'm sorry. I don't know where I know you from."

"I don't think you would remember me. We only met once, many years ago. It was at your Dad's wake. You were only a little kid. I worked with your Dad at the courthouse. My name is Walter, Walter Thomas."

"Oh, you were a clerk with my dad at the criminal courts in Hauppauge."

"Yes, that's right. I knew your dad pretty well. We used to go to lunch together all the time." Then he paused. "All the time… at least once a week."

"Really?"

"Oh, yea. He was a great guy, your old man."

"Yes, he was. Thank you, that's very nice to hear."

"I'm retired a few years now, I hate comin' to these things but I had to congratulate my old friend's daughter. Hey, you did okay for yourself, kid. Your father would be very proud."

Then Walter leaned in. "You know, between you and me," he whispered, "I don't see how he coulda done it. Your old man had no use for guns. At work, me and some of the other guys would give him hell, cause it seemed like he was scared of 'em."

"Really," Abby found herself saying again.

"Yep. Well, anyway, you never know, do ya? Hey, congrats, again, on getting Judge of the Year. I saw it posted on the court website and I had to drop by to say, 'hey.'"

"Thank you. That's very nice of you, Mr. Thomas."

"Call me Walter," he said. Then he leaned in again, a bit closer this time. "Are you still beating up all the lawyers that come into your courtroom?"

"How do you know that, Walter?"

"I'm retired, but I still hear things," he said with a sheepish grin.

"Yes," Abby answered returning the grin. "And most of them deserve it." Now Abby was leaning as well.

"Hope to see you again soon, Abby."

"Yes, me too." Abby paused. "Thank you for stopping by to say hello, Walter."

And with that, Walter disappeared into the large ballroom. He looked vaguely familiar. He was tall and very distinguished looking. Abby thought that in his younger days he must have been a very good-looking man.

Heck, he was handsome today, she thought.

He had salt and pepper hair; although more salt than pepper, and wore it vaguely parted on one side. His eyes were dark in color, almost black, and quite clear. Walter's smile was quick and bright and there was a certain roughness about his demeanor that was quite attractive to Abby. She liked rough men. They suited her lifestyle.

Abby was disappointed in her acceptance speech; it was choppy. She prided herself in her ability to speak in public. She felt as though this one was not up to her own self-imposed standards, but she was also aware that she was her own worst critic.

Otherwise the night went pretty much as she expected. The usual blur of overly polite lawyers, making sure that they were seen by Abby, extending congratulatory wishes and engaging in meaningless small talk. Abby's thoughts kept coming back to Walter, not surprisingly but more frequently then she expected.

"I wonder if he's left already," she said to herself as she handed the pretty young coat-check girl her claim stub.

"Can I help you on with that, your honor?"

Abby found herself smiling at the sound of that voice. She wasn't sure what it was but she could feel Walter's raspy words in different parts of her body; she best described it to herself as a tingle, but the feeling was indeed palpable.

"Yes, thank you," Abby responded, coyly, as she turned her head to face the voice.

Facing each other now and with the smile in that raspy voice clearly visible to Abby, she melted. The physical effect caused by Walter's voice was now compounded when he caught her eyes. She had become quite willingly, hypnotized by his deep, dark eyes.

"Can I walk you to your car?"

"Sure. Uh, I mean, no. My car is right there." Abby pointed, timidly to the car that was waiting for her, curbside.

"Well, then it'll be a short walk," Walter said as he lent Abby his arm. She took it without a word.

Walter signaled the door man with his hand, "I got it," he said not too softly as he opened the car door for Abby.

"Can I call you sometime, Abby?" Still in a trance, Abby nodded.

"Okay. What's your number," he asked as he produced his cell phone. "I'll put it in my phone."

"Okay," Walter said as he entered the last of the verbalized digits. "I'll call you so you have my number on your cell. Don't pick up. But pick up the next time I call, okay," he said with a smile and a wink.

Then Walter closed the car door and stood on the curb for a few moments as the car pulled away. Abby did not look back; she could not. She was enjoying the warmth that cloaked her body. That voice, those eyes; it was like parts of her were awoken for the first time. She rested her head back on the seat and looked up at the grey felt roof liner in the car until she could no longer keep her eyes from closing.

"We're here, Judge. We're at your house." The driver said, softly from the front seat.

It took Abby a second to realize where she was. The black car, the Judge of the Year dinner. Abby looked down at the plaque that was in her lap, her left hand still gripping it tightly.

"Oh, yes. Thank you."

The driver hopped out of the front seat, and opened her door. Abby took the driver's extended hand and slid out of the back seat. The cool autumn air finished what the polite driver had started. She was awake now.

"Thank you," Abby said softly as she handed the driver a couple of twenties.

"Thank you, Judge. You okay from here? I'll wait till you get in."

"Yes, I'm fine. Thanks again."

Any man would have rather enjoyed watching Abby's willowy silhouette climb the brownstone's stairs. The driver drove away only after Abby had closed her front door behind her.

Abby lay in her large canopy bed reviewing the night's events. She thought, as she smiled, of the only 'voice' and 'eyes' that made it worth reviewing. Still smiling she nodded off to sleep.

The sun shined brightly through the windows in Abby's bedroom. "Ten o'clock! Wow, I guess I was tired," Abby said softly to no one. In all but the winter months Abby liked to sleep in the nude. She just felt that clothes of any kind were very restrictive. She wanted to feel free when she slept. A bath robe, however, was never far away.

A cup of black coffee and a light breakfast was in order. Then as was a typical part of her Saturday morning schedule, a leisurely stroll to the local green market for fresh fruit and vegetables. Maybe a loaf of bread today, as well. She liked to get a French baguette once in a while, but only once in awhile. Abby knew that generally, avoiding bread was a key to keeping her hour glass figure.

This Saturday, like most, was to be delineated into three parts. The morning was for a few errands; the afternoon was dedicated to rest and relaxation, maybe a book or a nap. The evening, of course, was reserved for the man 'du jour.' Saturday night was date night.

Tonight's guy was one that she would see periodically. Abby was not sure what Frankie did for a living. When asked he would just say he was in the family business. She only asked once.

He was a bit of a control freak which was perfect for Abby's purposes. Men had one purpose in Abby's life and none fulfilled that purpose for very long. Abby's 'look' enabled her to be selective and she certainly was.

It was usually dinner and back to either his place or her place. Usually her place. She just felt more comfortable at her place. Frankie also had a nice place in Brooklyn and she had been seeing him long enough that his place was okay, too. He wanted what she wanted and nothing more.

The green market was only a few blocks away from Abby's brownstone. She inherited her home from her grandmother, not the one who helped raise her, her father's mother. She was a good woman. She was very stern, but quite loving in her own way.

Abby's building was a walk up that enjoyed two stories. All three bedrooms were on the second floor. One was on the smallish side and Abby liked to call that room her office. Although she rarely used it for anything except storing things that she would surely get to at another time.

The walls in Abby's home were predominantly white. However, the kitchen, which was not much larger than a galley, was painted in an off white to provide some warmth.

The living room wall that maintained the fireplace, had a solid marble mantle and built-in book shelves above. The mantel was made of dark, almost black, marble. Wainscoting covered the bottom half of the remaining living room walls. The top portion of those walls were covered with Abby's modest art collection. Two or three of which were painted by a distant cousin, who had long since passed on.

The windows in the living area were large and served to expose Abby to the vibrant city around her. From the dining area, which was off of the living room, the Brooklyn Bridge could be seen as could parts of lower Manhattan.

Although through smaller windows, Abby enjoyed a similar view in her bedroom. The bedroom was a large room but was decorated in such a way as to provide a warm feeling.

The walls were beige in color. The comforter displayed muted earthy tones with pillows in assorted matching colors. The window seat pillow was similar, just a bit bigger. The four-poster bed was of a natural oak hue, matching the other pieces of furniture.

At the foot of the four-poster bed was an antique trunk also of a light-colored wood that was weathered and worn. Only a metal plate remained where there once was a lock. However, other than the bed, it might have been Abby's favorite piece of furniture in the room, in part because of the history that it carried with it but also for the contents that it held.

Brooklyn Heights was a small community within a large borough. Abby felt both protected and anonymous by her surroundings. She felt very comfortable there.

Being a Brooklynite, Abby considered a car a luxury, but it was a luxury that she enjoyed. The LIRR would provide the transportation for Abby to fetch her car from her Aunt's garage in Huntington.

The hour or so train ride was about all Abby could tolerate. If it were any longer, the train would start to feel like a cage from which she needed to escape.

She liked to sit facing forward against the window in a two seater. Sometimes, she read the paper or a book but most times she just looked out the window at the sights that she had seen countless times before, daydreaming, always daydreaming.

She never brought work with her. She worked enough. She was the first judge in the courthouse in the morning and usually the last one to leave at night.

She researched and wrote many of her own decisions which was an atypical practice among the judges.

"That's why they invented law clerks," one of the older, gruffer judges would often say when he spotted Abby still toiling as he left the courthouse. Abby would look up and smile, then quickly return to her work.

Abby was a graduate of New York Law School, also in Manhattan. She graduated and she never looked back. Law School didn't matter to her. It was a necessary evil for her to accomplish her goal, a judgeship.

Her position on the Supreme Court Bench fit her personality perfectly. She was a born decision maker. She loved it, she thrived on it, it was who she was.

Abby poured herself a second cup of coffee as she reviewed the morning's errand list in her mind. The green market would be first. It almost always was. Weekend mornings were often tough on Abby. This one wasn't. She had gotten a good night's sleep.

I'll probably make up for it tonight, she thought to herself. *It is 'date night'* and she knew all too well what to expect from an evening with Frankie.

Sunlight dominated this Brooklyn morning as she walked the three blocks from her home to the market-place. *Everything looked especially fresh today,* she thought, walking from one table to the next.

The carrots looked more orange, the celery greener, and the apples a deeper red this morning. Abby picked up some vegetables for a stew that she was planning to prepare. She couldn't leave without picking up a couple of jars of homemade jam; they were on sale. "I can never pass up a good jam sale," she giggled to herself.

As was typical she would drop her newly purchased groceries off at her place before continuing on with her errands. And as was also typical, she would break off an end of the baguette to satisfy an urge that was no doubt precipitated by the aroma that the fresh loaf of bread provided during her three-block walk home.

Next stop was the dry-cleaners. John, the proprietor, was a friend. He was interested in becoming more than just Abby's friend and made his intentions known on more than one occasion, although less and less lately. Abby wasn't interested in John becoming anything more than what he already was, her friendly, neighborhood dry cleaner.

Abby had been 'around the block' as she would say, periodically, when the situation presented itself. She wondered to herself on more than one occasion if that were true or if it just gave her an internal justification for her thought process and more specifically for some of her actions.

She had however definitely been 'around that block' enough to know how to give a man that was interested in her a negative response without it seeming, even remotely, like a rejection. Most men didn't do well with rejection, no matter how slight, Abby thought, smiling softly.

"Good Morning, John! How are you today?" "Very well, Abby. How are you today?"

John made sure to use Abby's first name because she asked him in a whisper, while leaning into him, not to call her Judge in public. John remembered that conversation.

"I only have a few items today, John," Abby said while handing her friend her ticket.

John returned quickly with two light blouses and two dark skirts secured on hangers and neatly wrapped in plastic.

"Here you go, Abby. Shall I put this on your house charge?"

"Yes, please, John," Abby said as she reached up on the metal pole to gather her garments.

"Okay. Have a good day."

"You, too." Abby returned John's smile.

"He's just too nice," Abby said softly to herself when she was out of earshot. "I could never be with him."

The errand list was short today. *Just as well* she thought because she had bought a book off Amazon recently. It was one that one of the local attorneys had written and she wanted to start it before she took her Saturday afternoon nap.

Rarely did she feel as refreshed as when she awoke from a long weekend nap. She had just enough time to have a cup of tea before she had to jump in the shower.

A black pencil skirt and a soft, white blouse was her 'go to' outfit. Typically, with her 'uniform' she wore dark stockings. Sometimes, however, her legs remained bare but a pair of her many black high heels always finished off the outfit. She chose for this evening's meeting one of her favorite pair: plain black pumps.

Tonight, Frankie would be able to enjoy Abby's shapely legs without the black hose. Abby knew he would. She knew what he liked, and she aimed to please. *That was the whole idea,* she thought; *to please.*

Abby's afternoon tea was interrupted by a text message from Frankie. He wanted to meet at Jesse's Steakhouse; a restaurant close to Abby's home. She knew the reason for that request. Frankie was easy to read. Most men, she thought, were fairly easy to read.

She was sure it had something to do with the contents of the old trunk at the foot of her bed. She smiled at that thought. His plan was, obviously, a quick dinner and then back to her place. She nodded slightly as she sipped her tea and the smile never left her face.

She liked it when men took charge in her personal life. At least that's what she told her male companions, and for the most part, it was true. Tonight, though, she wasn't sure what she was feeling. She finished her tea and got ready for her shower.

She typically took a long, hot shower. The water temperature had to be hot enough to sting. She needed to feel something in the shower. She always needed to feel something. Abby lived to feel.

It was a large shower, large enough to comfortably accommodate two or three people. Abby liked to shower alone; it was a private place. More importantly, showering with another required a certain amount of tenderness and affection. Abby didn't have the inclination for such things.

She liked to use a fragrant body wash and a washcloth to lather it liberally on her body. After the conditioner had been gently and thoroughly messaged in her hair, she would shave whatever needed to be shaved. She carefully placed one foot at a time on the closest shower wall and shaved the uplifted leg. That process took only minutes.

A soft, soothing lotion would follow each shower. Her 'baby soft' skin was an attribute that each of Abby's lovers acknowledged and appreciated. The preparation for tonight's encounter did not differ from the others.

Abby got dressed quickly; no jewelry at all this evening. She was anxious to get to Jesse's Steakhouse. She wanted to be seated, having a drink, when Frankie arrived. Sometimes she liked to make an entrance; not tonight.

It had been a little while since she had been with Frankie. She liked him. She liked him about as much as she could like any man.

Frankie was already at Jesse's when Abby arrived. He was seated at the bar, far enough away that Abby was able to feel the many pair of eyes on her as she walked to where he was.

"Hi Abby. Nice to see you again. You look great!"

"Hi Frankie. Great to see you, too." A mutual peck on the cheek followed.

Frankie turned away from Abby to face the corner barstool that he had saved for her. The u-shaped bar at Jesse's was large enough to have its own room. It was an eclectically decorated restaurant that tried hard not to lose that New York steak house feel. Abby thought on more than one occasion that it tried too hard.

"Pinot Grigio, Abby?"

"Yes, that's right. Thanks."

"I thought we should have a drink before we sit down. Our reservation isn't until 7:00."

"That will be fine. Whatever you want, Frankie."

"That's the response I like, Abby. You know that," Frankie said with a slight grin. Then he turned and ordered Abby's glass of wine.

Abby felt smaller for a moment, less like Abby, or maybe more like Abby. She wasn't sure. "Thank you, Frankie," Abby said softly as he slid the glass of wine and its cocktail napkin in front of her. Frankie didn't respond. He just reached for his half full martini glass.

"I'll have another, please," Frankie said before putting his empty glass down. The bartender nodded once.

Turning his attention again toward Abby, he smiled and whispered, "You look great this evening."

"Thank you, Frankie. That's very nice of you to say." Abby looked down at her glass of wine on the bar. She didn't pick it up.

She just looked at and caressed the stem.

"I mean you look really nice tonight. Hot!"

Abby whispered, "Thank you," without looking up.

"C'mon, let's grab a table, so we can get back to your place," Frankie exclaimed as he stood up with newly delivered drink in hand, his head swiveling to locate a hostess.

"Great, they gave us our table." Frankie's comment was uttered only after they were comfortably seated at a small deuce against the wall. Abby nodded and smiled.

"You wanna get a bottle of wine? I'll feel like a big California cab tonight. I've had enough vodka." He pushed the martini glass aside. I shouldn't have ordered the second one. But it did hit the spot."

Abby just smiled and nodded. "A cabernet would be very nice, Frankie. Thank you."

"What are you thinkin' about for dinner tonight?" Abby opened her menu in response.

"I think you'll have a filet mignon today, medium rare and I will have the cowboy rib-eye. I'm hungry tonight." Frankie caught Abby's eyes again; his open-mouth smile allowed him to simultaneously lick his lips. Abby looked down again.

"Don't look away from me, ever! You know better than that." "I'm sorry,"

"You're sorry? That's it?"

"I'm sorry, Mr. Alberano.. Please forgive me"

"That's better."

"We'll have your best California Cab," Frankie said to the approaching waiter.

"Very good, Sir." The waiter turned to retrieve the bottle of wine.

"I see you're wearing what I like. That's good. That makes me happy." Frankie's smile was quick and contrived.

Abby just nodded and closed her menu.

The second bottle of wine came quickly. Abby had barely started her dinner when Frankie ordered it. Abby was not a big drinker especially of heavy red wines, but she had a glass or two.

The walk home was slow and deliberate. Abby needed it to be. She had to take back the evening.

"Well, thank you for a wonderful evening," Abby said softly as she turned away from her front door to face her date.

"What, no playtime tonight?" Frankie tried to allure Abby with his voice but he knew the answer before the question came out.

"No, not tonight," Abby whispered in as gentle a tone as was available to her at that moment. She just wasn't into 'playtime' tonight.

"I was really looking forward to diving into your 'toy chest,' this evening. You know, like last time." His latest plea was made while holding Abby's shoulder's gently.

"Maybe next time. I'm very tired tonight for some reason." Abby knew that the excuse was weak but, she also thought that for some reason, one was necessary.

"How bout a nightcap?" Frankie was dancing as fast as he could now. "No Frankie," Abby responded in a soft but stern tone.

"Yea, maybe next time." Frankie turned on his heels and very briskly walked away. Abby was left alone on the sidewalk, keys in hand, with her thoughts for a moment. The moment passed and she walked toward her front door.

Almost immediately when she stepped into her home Walter ran through her mind. She believed that a bit odd. Thoughts of him had not entered her mind since the awards night. *Well, that's not exactly true* she thought. Abby smiled.

CHAPTER 3

The rain clouds hid the morning sun. *Rainy Mondays, my favorite.* Abby spoke to herself often as she prepared her morning coffee. It was then when she first heard her voice each morning. Some mornings, she thought, it was more raspy than others. She rarely knew the reason and even less often was concerned; it seemed that by the time she arrived at the courthouse each morning she had a good voice. Abby's voice might be better described as commanding from the minute she took the bench.

Typically, Supreme Court Judges took the bench only for an occasional hearing or trial. It was the custom of most judges to avoid putting the black robe on at all costs. They were all elected to fourteen year terms so most paced themselves.

Abby was different. She loved the action. She took the bench as often as she could, often times standing behind her chair and challenging attorneys with relevant case law. She expected clear and concise arguments from lawyers and would accept nothing less.

Her reputation preceded her. Judge Polk's rulings were fair but to enter her courtroom was at best intimidating. An attorney dare not go before her unless fully prepared and even then many were reduced to stuttering advocates. Most walked out of Judge Polk's courtroom dissatisfied with either their performance, the outcome, or both.

"There's someone on the phone for you, Judge. He says he's an old friend," Lisa, the judge's secretary said as Abby passed by her desk. Her hand covered the receiver.

"I'll take it at my desk. Thank you."

"Okay." After a few words to the caller, Lisa put the call on hold. Lisa was an attractive woman in her late fifties, as with everyone before and since, life did not wait for Lisa. Although married once, for a short time, she was childless and now lived alone.

It could be reasonably assumed that she was a beautiful woman before the hands of time re-molded her body and the effects of smoking mildly distorted her face.

Lisa's straight blonde hair was all one length and barely reached her shoulders. Her eyes were bright and blue and soft when they needed to be.

She had been with the judge for some time. Abby liked having her around. Lisa's recurrent mood swings were less frequent now.

She was always efficient and now, a real pleasure to be around.

"Hello, this is Judge Polk. Can I help you?"

"Hi, Abby. It's your old friend Walter. I just called to see if you wanted to have lunch one day this week. Maybe get to know each other better."

Abby paused for a moment. "Well, that would be very nice. I'm not sure that I can make it this week. I'm supposed to start a trial tomorrow. I won't know my availability until later today. Can I call you later?"

"Yeah, sure. No problem. Let me know later. I'm around."

"Alright, then. I'll call you later today. Thank you for the call Walter."

Abby sat motionless for a moment after she returned the receiver to its holder, her mind racing, her eyes affixed straight ahead on nothing in particular.

"Hello, Judge Polk. It's a pleasure to meet you. My name is Sarah Roland."

"Won't you please sit down."

"Yes, thank you. I want to thank you again for giving me this opportunity to work with you this semester."

"It is our pleasure to have you join us. The students that have interned for us from Brooklyn Law School have all proven to be knowledgeable and quite helpful. I understand from your moot court professor, whom I have known for many years, that you did very well in the competition…"

"Yes, I was lucky enough to win," Sarah nervously interrupted.

"Yes, I heard. Anyway, as I was saying, I'm sure that you will do nothing to break that trend."

Judge Polk's chambers were large, the largest in the courthouse. Her chair was positioned so that her back was facing the large windows overlooking the bustling streets of Brooklyn. On the long wall to Abby's left were overstuffed bookshelves while degrees and citations covered the opposite wall. Across from the judge at her large oak desk sat three armchairs. However, most attorney conferences took place in her law clerk's, much smaller office next door.

Judge Polk much preferred most discussions with attorneys to be in open court. She liked to be wearing her robe when discussing issues with lawyers. And she almost always wanted discussions to be on the record. Off the record discussions could be held by her law clerk.

"Phillip, can you come in here for a minute, please?" The judge's voice was just loud enough for her law clerk in the next office to hear.

Moments later, a smallish, middle-aged man with conventional black glasses appeared in the judge's doorway. Phillip's tie seemed to always be loosened and the collar of his pink or white shirt unbuttoned. He never wore a suit jacket. He learned early on that it was unnecessary.

"Yes, Phillip, I trust that you have finished drafting the decision on the Jacoby motion, the one we spoke about last night."

"Not yet, Judge. It will be on your desk by the end of the day." "I'll expect it then, by 5:00 sharp. That'll be all, Phillip. Thank you." Phillip promptly departed.

"Judge, excuse me, but both the attorneys are here on the settlement conference," Lisa said after a brief knock on the door.

"Okay, I will be with them in a few minutes."

"Okay, Judge. I will have the court clerk tell them," Lisa said, having heard that same response from the Judge countless times before.

"Gentlemen, please sit down," Judge Polk said to the approaching attorneys about 15 minutes later.

"Have we made any progress in settling this matter?"

"Not really, Your Honor," one lawyer responded.

"No, Judge. We really haven't. I've come down substantially and counsel has not come up at all."

"Where are we, Gentlemen?"

"I came down from 650 to 300, Judge," the second lawyer quickly responded. "And counsel is still at 60."

"Sixty! Counsel, you are wasting my time! You need to go speak to your clients and tell them that they need to come up with more money—a lot more money. Tell them that the Judge sees their potential exposure as substantial. I'll give you 15 minutes."

"Yes, Judge," the first lawyer sheepishly replied. "I know my clients are not doing well financially, but I will do what I can."

"See you in 15 minutes, Gentlemen," Judge Polk responded closing the file on her desk.

"Judge, the two attorneys for this week's trial are here today, as you instructed. I believe they want to make an application."

"Okay, call the reporter. I'll be out as soon as she comes up." "Yes, Judge."

"Okay, call the case," Judge Polk ordered as she entered the courtroom and took her place on the bench.

"All rise. The honorable Justice Polk presiding."

"Please be seated. Call the case."

"Counsel on Deitrich vs Benchmark Inc… Appearances, please… Thank you."

"Good morning, gentlemen. Are we ready to go tomorrow?"

"No, Judge. I'm requesting an adjournment."

"You had better have a good reason, Counsel. This case has been marked ready for trial. The court is ready."

"Unfortunately, Judge, my wife's father suffered a serious heart attack just last night. He is in the ICU in a comatose state as we speak."

"I'm sorry to hear that, Counsel. We will pick a date in a month. Mr. Clerk, give us a date, please."

"November 15th"

"Alright Gentlemen, see you on the 15th. Be ready to try this case on that day. Check in the day before as is required by the rules of this part. Thank you, Gentlemen."

"Yes, Judge. Thank you."

"Thank you, Judge."

"Off the record. Counsel, approach. My best to your fatherin-law, Mr. Jameson."

"Thank you, Your Honor."

"See you in a month, Counsel."

Each attorney shot a quizzical look at the other as they left the courtroom. Judge Polk retreated to her chambers.

"Judge, the attorneys on the settlement conference are ready."

"Tell them I will be with them in a few minutes."

"Judge, you wanted to see me," Sarah asked. She entered chambers making barely a sound.

"Yes, Sarah. I'd like you to sit in on this settlement conference."

"Okay, Judge. Thank you."

"Have a seat over there. I will bring the attorneys in shortly."

"Come in Gentlemen. Have a seat."

"Thank you, Judge."

"Thank you, your honor."

"I hope you have more money, Counsel." The Judge's icy stare made the lawyer slump slightly in the leather tuft armchair.

"Yes, Judge. Another 20. I have 80 now."

"Will that do it Counsel?" The icy stare was transposed to the other attorney.

"I'm afraid not..."

"I didn't think so. What's your demand, 300?"

"Yes, Judge and as you know, I came down substantially in an effort to settle this case. I can't come down anymore, Judge. I'm sorry."

"Okay, gentlemen. I guess we are trying this case. Phillip, give them a month. And Counsel, we are trying this case in a month. No excuses!" Both attorneys replied, "Yes, Judge" almost in unison." December 6th," Phillip said without looking up from his datebook.

"See you on December 6th, Gentlemen."

As the three men scurried out of chambers, Judge Polk said quietly, "Sarah, I'd like you to stay behind for a few minutes."

"Yes, Judge. Of course."

Phillip did not look back. He followed the lawyers out of the room and closed the door behind him.

"Sarah, sit down here, where the attorneys were sitting."

"Okay, Judge Thank you."

"I would like to get to know you a little bit better." Sarah smiled. "You are a little older to be in law school, aren't you?"

"Yes, Judge. I didn't go to law school right out of college. I worked in the research field for a little while. I started law school in my early 30s."

"Research? Where did you work?"

"I did work for a clinical psychologist."

"Psychology? Really? Do you have an undergraduate degree in psychology?"

"Yes, I do. I graduated from Columbia."

"Oh, that's very interesting. What made you decide to go to law school?"

"I thought my education would help me in defense work. I would, actually, like to work for the public defender's office. I think my background is best suited for that kind of work."

"You sound very sure of yourself. I like that. You remind me of my Mom. She was like that, very confident and sure of herself. Even some of your mannerisms remind me of my mom."

"Is your mom still with us, Judge?"

"No, I'm sorry to say that she is not." Then the judge paused and seemed to look away for a moment. "She passed away a couple of years ago, but I think about her every day," she said quietly, still focused on the wall behind Sarah.

"I'm sorry to hear that, Judge. My condolences."

"Thank you. We were very close." The judge snapped back into focus. "Well, it was nice to get to know you a bit better, Sarah."

"Yes, Judge, it was very nice talking with you as well. I'd better get back to work now," Sarah responded after hesitating briefly.

"Thank you, Sarah."

"Yes, Judge." The judge's gaze became fixed on nothing in particular.

The dementia came upon Abby's mother, Dorothy, slowly at first. She had suffered from hearing loss for some time. She just couldn't find a hearing aid that she was comfortable using. Abby had tried every audiologist in the area and countless hearing aids. It was difficult to determine exactly when or if the hearing loss morphed into dementia.

Up until the last few weeks she always seemed to pass every test that her doctor gave her.

'What is today's date?' 'Who is the President?' 'What town do you live in?' She answered them all correctly, every time, until she didn't. Then the doctor just stopped asking. It was time then for 24/7 care. Even that did not prevent numerous trips to the hospital for dehydration and other similar maladies. Each hospital stay was followed by a stay at a rehab center. Then home again.

Abby, meanwhile, would make sure she stopped by her mom's condo at least a few times a week to spend time and check her status.

The home health care aids were rotated every two weeks and paid in cash; cash only.

Abby's mom passed after spending a week in a coma state at home in a hospice setting. Abby remembered that the need for hospice came suddenly.

Dorothy deteriorated quickly right before Abby's eyes. Abby had recalled a few times toward the end when her mom would not know who she was. Then the last time she saw her mom, which was the day before she fell into a coma, she could not acknowledge Abby's presence at all. It was heartbreaking.

Abby buried her mother on a late winter's day. Spring was beginning to awaken. The sun's warmth, so long absent, dominated the short time at the cemetery.

Abby's tears were gone. There were no more. It had been weeks and weeks of crying. She just didn't have any more to shed. She stood stoically during the service, her head bowed, and she spoke to no one.

After the luncheon, on the day of the funeral, she returned to her Brooklyn apartment alone. There, she found some more tears. She sat in the dark and cried the cry of a grief-stricken daughter.

As night fell upon her Brooklyn home, she dried her eyes long enough to take herself out for long walk. The cool fresh air felt good. It was during that walk that she realized for the first time that for the remainder of her life she was alone. She had no sisters or brothers, no family of her own and now she had lost her mom and her best friend.

"Sarah, I would like to take you to lunch today; maybe we can talk some more."

"Okay, Judge. That would be very nice. Thank you."

"Be ready to leave about 1:15. We can talk some more."

"Fine, Judge. Thank you." The judge's movements designated Sarah's instant dismissal. In spite of that, Sarah lingered a few moments before turning and walking out.

Abby pulled her cell phone from her oversized purse that she kept in a bottom draw in her desk.

"Hello Walter. It's Abby. How are you?" Abby couldn't wait until tomorrow to make the call.

"Great, Abby. How are you?"

"I'm doing very well. Thank you. I just called to tell you that I'm clear for lunch this week. I thought I would let you know as soon as I knew."

"So, no trial."

"No trial. It was adjourned."

"Okay. What day is good for you?"

"Let's shoot for Friday if it's all the same to you."

"Friday is good for me. Remember, sweetie, I'm retired. How 'bout Johnnie's BBQ Pit? It's a BBQ joint not far from the courthouse. Do you know it?"

"Yes. I do. That sounds like fun. I've only been there once. It was some time ago for a retirement party, I think. Let's go there. It should be fun." Abby pursed her lips as she waited for a response. "I said fun. Did I just say fun," she whispered with her hand tightly wrapped around the receiver.

"Sounds good. What time is good for you, sweetie?"

"I should be able to get there by 1:00."

Great. See you then. Looking forward to it."

Abby paused. "Me too," she said before she hung up the phone. She thought that her response came out softly, almost timidly, but she nevertheless was looking forward to the lunch.

xxxxxxxxxx

"Sarah, are you ready to go," The judge's question was asked in a manner that did not contemplate a response.

"Yes, Judge. I'm ready."

"Okay. Let's go."

"I thought we would go to the diner on the corner. The food is pretty good there and the service is fast; so, we can get back to court quickly."

The judge shot a smile to Phillip as she headed to the back elevator. Phillip barely returned the smile. Most of his smiles between 9 and 5 were insincere.

"It's just around the corner; this way." Abby pointed to the left with her body. Sarah never missed a beat. She made sure to walk beside Abby. Sarah was not a follower.

"Okay. I think I might know the place. I went to lunch at a nearby diner after my interview for the internship."

"Yes, it's a pretty popular place. It's right at the end of the block. Why don't you lead the way."

"All right. I will," Sarah replied, as she turned her head to face the judge who was already a step or two behind.

"The manager asked, in a thick Greek accent. "Booth or table," he continued turning to grab the menus.

"It's up to you." The judge was responding to a glance from

Sarah. Sarah said nothing.

"We'll take a booth, please," the judge said.

The manager shot the judge a look.

"Follow me." He placed the menus on the table and quickly turned away from the booth by a window.

"What are you thinking about having, Judge?"

"Please, don't call me Judge when we are in public. Abby is fine. Thanks."

"Oh, right. I'm sorry, Abby." They exchanged warm smiles.

"I don't know what to order," the judge answered behind an open menu. "Everything looks so good."

"I'm gonna have a hamburger," Sarah said, closing her menu. "And maybe a cup of soup if they have something I like."

"Can I get you something to drink?" The waiter's accent was nearly as heavy as the manager's.

"I'll have a coke, please." Abby said.

"Do you know what you want to order," he asked.

"Yes, I think so. What kind of soup do you have today?"

"They're listed here." The waiter pointed to the portion of the Judge's menu which listed the specials.

"Okay. Thanks. I'll have a cup of Manhattan clam chowder and a hamburger, medium rare. Please."

The waiter removed the menu from the table.

"So how long have you been on the bench, Abby," Sarah asked in a soft voice.

"This is my 13th year. I have to run for re-election next year. It goes fast."

"Really? It's a fourteen year term for Supreme Court Justices?"

"Yes. Seems long but it flies by and before you know it…" Abby's voice tailed off.

Abby, do you like what you do?"

"Most days. Things have been a little strange in chambers lately."

"How do you mean?"

"Things have been done and said, recently, that make me question the loyalty of some of the people around me."

"Really? Would you like to give me an example?"

"I can't think of anything right now," Abby responded after a pause.

Silence took its turn at the table until the soup arrived.

"I did make some enemies in the defense bar when I sat in the criminal part for a few years. I was known as the 'hangin judge.' I sentenced defendants to what I thought they deserved." The judge paused briefly.

"If they took a plea, I usually went along with the deal. But if they were convicted after trial, I threw the book at them. Criminal defense lawyers didn't like that."

"How does that hurt you now? You're in the civil part."

"Yes, but it could hurt my chances of getting the conservative endorsement that I need to get reelected."

"That doesn't seem fair, Abby. You would think the Conservatives would be in favor of heavy sentences."

Abby chuckled "Fair, this is politics, where fairness is rarely contemplated. Besides, it's how the game is played nowadays. Many defense attorneys are members of the Conservative party and they have a lot of pull. Just keep your eyes open around chambers. "A lot of whispering and talking behind closed doors. They think I don't notice, but I do."

Now it was Sarah who hesitated. She continued eating her chowder as she listened to Abby. When she had finished she put her spoon down, wiped her mouth with the white paper napkin on her lap and leaned back slightly.

"Okay," she said. "I will, Abby."

The judge was feeling very vulnerable, and Sarah knew that the less said to expose those feelings, the better. Now, Sarah asked herself, *were any of these feelings warranted?*

Sarah knew that she was perfectly capable of getting some answers. That was not the only question she had though.

"Thank you for lunch, Abby."

"You're very welcome, Sarah. It was my pleasure. Just remember what I asked of you today."

Sarah nodded. "I will," she said.

Few words accompanied the two women on the walk back to the courthouse. Sarah occasionally glanced over toward the judge who each time was looking straight ahead. She had a determined gaze. It was the walk of someone walking alone, Sarah thought.

CHAPTER 4

Abby's week went exactly as planned; no surprises. There rarely were in Abby's work life. Everything was within her control. Friday, however, did not come as quickly as she would have liked. But when it finally did, Abby was ready for her BBQ lunch.

She always dressed well. She dressed like she thought a supreme court justice should dress; distinguished but feminine. She wouldn't let anyone forget that she was an attractive woman.

That Friday morning, she dressed with her luncheon engagement in mind. She was careful not to wear a white blouse. *After all, they were having BBQ,* she thought.

"Good morning, Phillip."

"Good morning, Judge."

"Where's Lisa this morning?"

"She's running a little late this morning, Judge," Phillip responded without delay. He was in a hurry to get something from the cafeteria to go with his morning coffee. The judge watched him get on the elevator.

"Sarah, please come into my chambers as soon as you can."

"Yes, Judge."

Sarah followed the judge into her chambers.

"Hi, Sarah. Come in. Sit down." The judge was seated behind her desk with her large, black-framed reading glasses resting securely on the bridge of her nose. The look resembled, to some degree, Bridget Moynahan in Blue Bloods.

In a tone barely audible, she asked, "Well Sarah, have you heard anything?"

"Yes, Judge. As a matter of fact, I have."

"What did you hear?"

Sarah leaned forward just slightly so that the judge would think that the intern thought it was important. It was to be a gauge for Sarah.

"Judge, I heard that you might have some difficulty securing the Conservative line in next year's election. Apparently, you made more than a few enemies when you were sitting in the criminal part."

"Yes, I know I upset some lawyers but I did what I thought was right," Abby leaned back in her chair and looked up at the ceiling as she spoke. "And I wouldn't do anything differently."

"How important is the conservative line for you to get re-elected?"

"Very important! I'm sure Phillip told you that, too," Abby leaned forward in her chair as she spoke; her eyes now fixed on Sarah.

Sarah did not lean back in her chair, and she did not say anything right away. She just looked at the judge for a moment or two. However, she knew exactly what was expected of her.

"What can I do to help?"

"I'm glad you asked," the judge said leaning back again and smiling contently. "I have a meeting with the conservative leader next week and I want you to come with me. I need your read on the meeting."

"Yes, of course, Judge. I will be happy to go with you."

"I'll tell you this, if I get elected again…when I get elected again, I will definitely get a new law man. Phillip is out." Then, she said in a whisper as she turned away from Sarah, "I detest disloyalty."

"I'm sorry, Judge. I missed that."

"I said that, 'I don't like disloyal people.' I won't have them around me." She was now looking directly at Sarah and her tone was louder and more threatening than a few moments earlier.

"Oh. I see."

"Did he tell you that he's trying for judgeship himself? And in doing so he's going to need the conservative's backing as well."

"He wouldn't be running against you, would he?"

"No, no, Family Court. However, when these deals are made some people have to be left out. It depends on the agreement that's been made between the leaders. I cannot be left out and I won't be. You can be rest assured of that." Her tone was only slightly less threatening.

Sarah said nothing. She sat silently and studied the judge's face. The judge had turned her face toward the open file on her desk. Her subterfuge of being busy was her way of putting an exclamation point on her last statement, while at the same time dismissing Sarah.

"Well, Judge, I'm going to back to work now. We can talk later if you like."

"Right," replied the judge without lifting her head.

xxxxxxxxxx

The BBQ place was jumping. Walter was at the relatively small bar when Abby arrived.

"Hi, Abby. Nice to see you again. Not many stools at this bar. Here, grab mine while I check on a table for us."

"Hello, Walter. Okay. Thank you."

"Order a drink while I'm gone. Not sure what you like, otherwise it would have been sitting here waiting for you." Walter smiled and threw some money on the bar before he turned away to find the hostess.

After only a few minutes Walter returned, still smiling, and announced that, 'they have a table ready for us.' He collected his change. He left a tip and his glass of beer and thanked the bartender. The hostess equipped with two menus lead the new couple to their waiting table.

"This is a nice table. Let's get down and dirty with a couple of baby backs," Walter offered. Abby giggled.

"Yes, let's," she said, feeling more relaxed than she had felt in some time.

"No menus needed. We will have two racks, please," Walter said to the approaching waitress.

"Full racks?" she asked without looking up.

"Oh yea, full racks, two of them. And I'll have another beer too. Do you need another glass of wine?" "No, I'm good," Abby responded.

"Okay, then. Two full racks and what kind of beer were you drinking?"

"Heineken, please."

"Okay. I'll be right back with it."

"Thank you," Walter said, turning his attention to Abby. "Do you have a busy afternoon?"

"No, pretty light day today. How about you? What do you do with your time now that you're retired?"

"Well, I play golf when I can. I still go to the range pretty often."

"The driving range?"

"No, the target range," Walter said with a smile. "I still like to shoot. You know, target practice. Pistols."

"I'm familiar with pistols, Walter," Abby answered, returning the smile.

"I also spend a lot a time on my bike. I have a Harley; full dress. I take it upstate when I can and I find that I can pretty often. I ride with a few guys. We're all retired so we have plenty of time."

"I'm familiar with Harleys too." Her short titter ended with another sip of wine.

"Maybe we can go for a ride one day. What da ya say?" "Sure. Why not? Sounds like fun."

"Believe me, Abby; it will be fun. You'll fall in love with it. It's a great feelin'; a feelin' of freedom, like no other."

"I don't feel free very often," Abby replied softly.

"Well then, this is just what the doctor ordered, isn't it?"

"I guess so," Abby said in a slightly raised voice.

"How 'bout tomorrow? We'll get up early and head up to Reinbeck. It's supposed to be a beautiful day. Walk around the town, have a little lunch, then come home. I'll have you home by 4:00." Abby thought, *my Friday night plans would have to be changed.*

"I don't know anything about you, Walter. Where do you live? Do you have kids? Oh yea, and are you married?"

"I'm widowed. My wife died a couple of years ago. I do have a son. I also have a daughter-in-law and a grandson. My son is married and is living just outside D.C. He works for the federal government, in some capacity. I'm really not sure what he does.

"Oh, how nice. How old is your grandson?"

"He's six now; getting big. He's in the first grade already." The lilt in her lunch date's voice, while he discussed his grandson, endeared him to Abby.

"Can I let you know about tomorrow later this afternoon?"

"Sure, you can. I know, I kinda sprung it on ya. Sorry, later is fine."

xxxxxxxxxx

"How was your lunch, Judge," Phillip asked almost immediately as Abby entered Lisa's outer office to chambers.

"It was fine, very pleasant. Thank you."

The Judge entered her inner chambers and sat behind her desk.

"Please have a seat, Sarah." The Judge's eyes followed Sarah as she sat in one of the leather tuffed chairs that faced the judge.

"I can't believe how much you remind me of my Mom. You even wear your hair like she wore hers. It was the same color as yours and she always wore it in a ponytail like you do."

"Yes, Judge. It's just easier this way."

"And your mannerisms, it's amazing! I know that you've only been here for a couple of weeks but…"

"Judge, I don't mean to interrupt, but I've only been here a week."

"Really? It seems longer, like we've known each other for a longer period of time. That brings me to my question. Just let me figure out how to say it. Gimme a minute."

The judge leaned back in her chair. She stared at the ceiling for a moment, then at the wall behind Sarah for what seemed like an hour.

Sarah was past the point of feeling uncomfortable. Maybe the judge was right; they did seem to know each other for more than one week.

"I like to be dominated in the evening. As you know, Sarah, I make many important decisions during the day, so at night, on my personal time, I like to be dominated by the men I date and I date many men."

"That's interesting, Judge. Well, maybe, not so much. What's interesting is that you're telling me this."

"It's nothing crazy. Not like 50 shades or anything. I just like to be told what to do. I don't want to make any decisions."

Sarah stayed silent, listening and waiting for the question that she suspected was not forthcoming.

"Sometimes I allow myself to be tied up, but typically not, just ordered around. I have no say and if I do say anything, a hand quickly covers my mouth. Those are the rules going in. Of course, I make the rules, but I don't break them. I wouldn't dare."

"Do you think that's a wise way to conduct your personal life, Judge? I mean a person in your position. You, you have a lot to lose; a lot to lose," Sarah repeated.

"I can't help myself. It's the only way I know."

"Well, then be careful, Judge. "Things can very easily get out of hand."

"'Careful', defeats the whole purpose." The Judge smiled and fixed her sight past Sarah again.

Abby's mind wondered to a time before her mom got sick. She remembered one particular conversation in her mom's condo. She was explaining to her mom the specifics of her political posturing. Early on,

Abby knew that she wanted to be a judge and she made it known to anyone who would listen.

Her mom always listened and ardently followed step by step her daughter's journey to achieve that goal.

"Be careful, honey. You're playing with fire."

"I can't get it done unless I do it this way, Mom."

"But, it sounds to me like you're using one party against the other."

"No, Mom, not really. I'm just making sure that I get the cross endorsement that I need to win. I know what I'm doing."

"I'm sure you do, honey. Just remember, politics can be a dangerous game," her mom replied, with a reassuring smile. The same smile that helped Abby get through most of the difficult times in her life.

"Yes, 'careful' defeats the whole purpose," Abby whispered. Sarah kept her eyes on the judge but said nothing.

"I'm sure that you know what you're doing, Judge. Just remember, what you've described to me can become a dangerous game and you have a lot to lose."

Abby, breaking free from her trance, responded, softly. "Thank you for your input, Sarah. I will take it under advisement." Abby's smile did not leave her lips until she suggested to Sarah that she return to work. Sarah exited the judge's chambers in silence. Abby did not look up from her desk to observe Sarah's short, over-the-shoulder glance.

xxxxxxxxxx

"Walter is on the phone, Judge."

"Okay, I'll take it."

"Hi Abby, Walter here. You told me to call the middle of the week, so I waited till Wednesday, can't get any more middle than this."

Abby giggled and said, "Glad to hear from you, Walter."

"Sorry, you couldn't make it last Saturday, but, like I said, there'll be other days."

"Sorry I couldn't make it as well. I knew I was going to have a late night on Friday, plans with some people from out of town that I couldn't change." *Maybe I shouldn't have said that. How believable is it?*

"No worries. Next time. How 'bout dinner this week?"

"I'd like that."

"How's Friday? Are your friends still in town?"

"No, they're gone," Abby responded without thinking twice.

"Great. I'm glad to hear that. I'll pick you up at seven." Walter responded in a light tone.

"Okay. I guess that'll be alright. I usually meet men out."

"C'mon, I'm not just any man. What's your address?"

"I guess that's true; you're not just any man." She smiled at that thought.

After Abby said goodbye and hung up the phone, she quickly and for the first time realized that she was going on a 'date' Friday night and she rather liked the idea.

"And this would be different," she said softly to herself. "This would be just a normal date."

"Remember, Sarah, today is the lunch with Dave Jenkins," Abby said as soon as Sarah entered her chambers.

"Yes, Judge. I remembered. What time are we meeting him?" "Well, as I said, we are meeting him at his office first. Then we are going out to lunch. I should say he is taking us to lunch." The door to Phillips office was closed.

Phillip's office was about one third of the size of the Judge's chambers, quite possibly even smaller. The wall on the left, as you walked in and faced his desk, contained a few degrees and citations. The top of Phillip's desk was covered with undecided motions of varying thickness.

Two additional and unyielding motion stacks of maximum height sat on the window sill behind his desk. They partially eclipsed a photograph of Phillip and his wife seated at a large round table at a wedding of a friend.

On the right was a signed photograph of Tom Seaver, Phillip's favorite Met. Right next to that photo was one of Phillip and the Judge on a much happier day in the fairly recent past. He found himself looking at that photo much less these days.

"Where's his office, Judge?" Sarah turned her head to ask the judge as they started out from the courthouse.

"We're meeting him at the Delphi Diner. He called and changed the plan."

Abby knew that wasn't necessarily a good sign but Sarah didn't need to know that, at least not right now. The meeting was still on and that was a positive indication. Abby would take anything she could get at this point.

"Hi, Dave. It's nice to see you again."

"Listen Abby, I have some bad news for you. We have worked out an endorsement deal with your party that does not include you."

"Boy, Dave, you get right to it, don't you? I barely sat down. Can I ask why?"

"Of course. You know I've always been honest with you. I want to get that family court slot filled and Phillip has some friends in the democratic party that I might need. As you might know I want to run my wife for a Supreme Court spot that should open up next year."

"Where does that leave me?"

"You made a lot of enemies when you sat in a criminal part for a couple of years. I'm sure that you know that. Some of these people still have a lot of juice. I can't afford to make those people my enemies as well, especially with my wife running next year."

"Well, you must know that I'm very disappointed. Is there anything I can do to change your mind, Dave?" Abby noticed Sarah looking at Dave, barely flinching at the judge's question.

The judge felt cornered in the booth by Sarah and across from Dave. She had both hands wrapped around her cup of coffee. A coy smile never left her lips and her eyes were now fixed on Dave.. After a pause, Dave responded. "I'm sorry, Abby, there isn't. The decision has been made."

"Then, you will have to excuse us. It looks like I have my work cut out for me to win this thing in November. We'd better get started."

Dave shot the judge a quizzical glance. "I understand, Abby. Good luck."

"Thank you," Abby replied, while standing next to Sarah and looking down at the still seated conservative leader.

"And thanks for the cup of coffee."

Sarah turned and followed Abby out. Once outside on the downtown Brooklyn street, Abby turned to Sarah and said, "what do ya think?"

"Well, yes, Abby. I think that you can be sure of not getting the conservative endorsement."

"Oh, that's where you're wrong Sarah. I will get the endorsement. One way or the other, I will get it."

Then the judge stopped and looked up and around a bit. "Nice day today, don't you think?"

"Yes, Abby it is. It's a very nice day."

"You can call me Judge again, since we're alone now."

Abby started ahead to the courthouse and as she did, she made sure to warn her intern not to speak about these conversations to anyone. For the remainder of that silent walk back to the courthouse, Sarah couldn't help but periodically gaze at the Judge.

xxxxxxxxxx

"Dave, I'd like to meet with you for a few minutes on Saturday morning if possible." Abby made the call as soon as she was behind closed doors in her chambers.

"Okay, Abby if you think we have something to talk about. I'm usually there about 10:00. Why don't you stop by then?"

"Thank you, Dave. I'll see you at 10 on Saturday morning." The judge made a second call immediately upon her making a Saturday appointment with the county conservative leader. It was a call that had not even entered her mind a few minutes earlier.

"Hi, Walter. Is that invitation for a glass of wine at your place still open?"

"Sure. When did you want to drop by?"

"How about tonight?"

"You got it; just give me a time."

"I'll be leaving here about 5:30…"

"…I'll see you at 6:00 then; looking forward to it."

"Make it 6:30. I want to stop by my place to freshen up. I'm looking forward to it as well, Walter."

"Okay, see you then."

Abby knew she looked good when she ascended the steps to Walter's walk up. She knew she looked good most days and almost every evening. She stood at his door barelegged, in a black skirt that was shorter than was typical for her and high heels that were a bit too high. To finish the look, Abby hooked one less button on her shear white blouse than usual.

Abby took a deep breath and rang the bell twice. The door was opened almost immediately. Walter stood smiling.

"C'mon in, Abby. You look great. Glad you called."

"Thank you. So am I." Abby wore her evening smile.

A hug and a very brief kiss on the lips greeted Abby once inside the door. Abby wanted the kiss to last longer.

A warm, comfortable living area opened to a small dining room and well-appointed kitchen. Two tall, sparkling wine goblets and an open bottle of Pinot Grigio waited in an ice bucket on the kitchen island.

"Let 'me pour the wine, then we can sit in the living room."

"Okay." Abby smiled again as she noticed Walter looking her up and down. *I'm glad I stopped home to 'freshen up.'*

Abby, with her hands clasped behind her back, wandered over to a floor-to-ceiling bookshelf in the living area. She stood with her legs apart and hands on her hips, perusing some of the titles. She turned away quickly.

"I hope you like this wine; it's one of my favorites. Everything alright?"

"Yes, fine. Why?"

"You just look a little preoccupied, that's all."

"No, I'm fine. Just was thinking about one of my cases. That's all."

"No business talk tonight. I won't allow it."

"Okay," Abby said with a smile.

"C'mon over here and join me on the sofa."

Abby took notice as to what the acceptable distance to sit next to Walter on the sofa would be, and she sat a bit closer. When she crossed her legs a fair amount of thigh was exposed. Walter's eyes lost Abby's eyes for a moment but found her lap. Abby smiles coyly.

A perfunctory toast completed, he was able to steal yet another look at Abby's exposed upper thighs when he followed his glass to the coffee table as he placed it down. Abby missed none of it.

"You have great legs, Abby. I hope you don't mind me sayin' that."

She not only didn't mind, she expected it.

"No, not at all, Walter. It's very nice of you to say. A woman can't hear that kind of stuff enough. At least, this woman can't." Abby lifted her glass and smiled. Walter reached for his glass again and raised it to meet Abby's.

"You're my kind of girl," he said softly.

He then leaned in to kiss Abby. Her soft, full lips were waiting. It was a longer, more luscious kiss than Walter had expected. She had him and she knew it.

He couldn't help but stroke her thigh as the kisses continued.

Her skin was smooth and her thighs were strong and willing. He gently pushed her back so her head rested on the arm of the couch. The empty wine glass fell from her finger tips on to the area rug that surrounded the table on which she attempted to place it.

Her head tilted back as Walter kissed her neck. He positioned himself between her partially open legs. She could feel him through his pants.

C'mon, Baby girl, let's go inside," he said between short heavy breaths.

Abby jerked up to a sitting position as she pushed Walter off of her. She pulled her skirt down as far as it would go and joined her knees together.

"What's wrong, Abby? What happened?"

Abby fixed her hair as she stood up. "I have to go. I'm sorry. I just have to go."

"Okay," Walter answered, still seated looking up at Abby as she started for the door. "Let me walk you to the door."

"No, it's alright. I can find it. Good night."

Abby grabbed her pocketbook from the stool in the kitchen and left Walter sitting on the sofa with his mouth slightly agape.

CHAPTER 5

The next day was Thursday; motion day in Judge Polk's part. It was typically a very busy day in her part. Motions came pouring into the courthouse like mail to a post office. The volume might not be equivalent, but the consistency was. They just kept coming.

The day was filled with settlement conferences and oral arguments. Phillip tried to settle cases in his office while the judge listened to oral arguments from the bench. She was well prepared to listen to these arguments for two reasons.

The first is that she researched nearly every motion that was on her calendar for oral argument and the second is many of the issues that were to be argued before her she had heard and resolved in the past.

Most times she would stand behind her chair on the bench and question each attorney regarding relevant case law and how it applied. God help the attorney who was not prepared. That was one thing for which Judge Polk had very little patience.

Most attorneys were frantically reviewing their file and consulting with their iPads while waiting for their case to be called. This was a typical Thursday in Judge Polk's part.

This day the judge put her hand up to stop an attorney, who was trying to make a precedent setting legal argument, in mid-sentence. "Excuse me, Counsel... Is that Jason Peters who just walked into my courtroom," she said loudly to an attorney who was looking for a place to sit in the back of her courtroom.

"Yes, Judge," the startled Mr. Peters responded.

"Come up here, Mr. Peters. Approach the bench, please. Excuse me, Counsel," she said in a softer voice while facing the two lawyers who stood before her.

"Yes, Judge," they both seemed to respond in unison. The lawyers stepped away from the bench.

"How are you, Mr. Peters? It's nice to see you again."

It was the first time that most of the lawyers in her courtroom that day had ever seen Judge Polk smile. Those, that is, who took the time from their files and i-pads to observe this exchange.

"Nice to you see as well, your Honor."

"What can I do for you, today," the judge asked still sitting behind her high-backed chair.

"Judge, I'm just here to check on a case that's not on your Honor's calendar today; just wanted to check with the clerk when you left the bench."

"Nonsense. Mr. Clerk, can you help Mr. Peters with whatever he needs. Thank you."

"Thank you, Judge." Jason Peters approached the clerk with the index number scribbled on piece of scrap paper in hand.

"Okay, Gentlemen. You can approach now and finish your argument. I hope that you both took this time to refresh your notes."

These words compelled all heads in the courtroom to lower into their respective files again.

"Where were we, gentlemen? Oh, yes. We were discussing why neither of you had read 'Jackson vs. Longfellow Inc.'; a case on which your case will probably turn."

More than a few sets of attorney's eyes followed Jason Peters as he got what he needed from the clerk and proceeded out of the courtroom.

"Did you get what you needed, Mr. Peters?"

"Yes, Judge. Thank you."

When the judge returned to her chambers on that late Thursday afternoon, she remembered that she still hadn't made a phone call that she needed to make before Friday. *Damn it, it could wait till tomorrow.*

"Walter, hi, it's Abby. Unfortunately, I can't make it tonight. Sorry for the late notice." She didn't think she owed him any more than that. Abby didn't think she owed him anything.

"I'm sorry to hear that, Abby. Is everything all right? You left in a hurry the other night. I was just wondering that's all."

"Everything is fine. I just can't make it tonight, that's all."

"Okay. How 'bout tomorrow night. I'll pick you up the same time." Abby did not answer.

"Hello. Did I lose you? Are you there, Abby?"

"I'm here. Not sure about tomorrow yet. I've gotta go now. Call me in the morning."

xxxxxxxxx

"Hello, Abby. Come on in." David was always respectful to Abby. For the first time, this Saturday morning Abby was questioning his sincerity.

"Hello David. Hello Rita." Abby knew why David had asked his assistant to be there this Saturday morning. No matter, she wasn't going down that road.

"Can we talk for a few minutes alone, David?"

Rita looked up from the papers she was shuffling as she stood by the side of David's desk. She looked at Abby, then David. David nodded and Rita walked out past Abby who was not yet seated. Abby did not take her eyes off David, but she felt Rita's stare. Rita closed the door behind her.

"Please sit down, Abby."

"Thank you."

"How can I help you, today?"

"I think you know, David."

"I'm sorry, Abby but I mentioned the last time we met; the decision has been made."

After a short pause David continued. "And please remember that I'm a married man and I don't want to have to ask Rita to return."

"I was hoping this would change your mind," Abby said softly, as she reached into her oversized pocketbook and pulled out a large white envelope. It was crumpled and tightly wrapped by a large rubber band.

"Here's 50,000 reasons why you should change your mind." She gently placed the envelope on David's desk.

David put the fingers of both hands on top of the envelope and slid it to the end of the desk in front of Abby. The motion forced him to lean in. Then he said very quietly, "make it 100,000 reasons and we'll talk. This is Brooklyn, not Suffolk County. Now put that away."

Her eyes firmly affixed on David's face, she quickly stuffed the envelope in her bag which was now on her lap.

"I will see you soon."

"I have no doubt, Abby."

"I want that Judgeship."

"I know you do."

Abby got up to leave. After a few steps, she reached to open the office door, then turned only her head.

"See you next Saturday, Mr. Jenkins," she said in barely a whisper.

xxxxxxxxxx

"Sorry to bother you on a weekend, Sarah. But I needed to talk to you."

"It's no bother, Judge. You can call anytime."

"I was hoping you would say that. Are you alone?"

"Yes, Judge. I live alone. I thought you knew that."

"Yes, I guess I forgot. Please call me Abby."

"Okay, Abby. What's on your mind?"

"Nothing, really. I just wanted to say hi."

After a brief hesitation, Sarah said, "Well, that's nice, Abby. It's always nice to hear from you."

"What are you doing today, Sarah?"

"Not too much. Just some laundry and maybe a little reading."

"You're not going out tonight? It's Saturday night."

"No, Abby. I don't go out much. I don't seem to have the time."

"You're not seeing anyone?"

"No, not really. No one steady since my husband passed away."

"Oh, I'm sorry. I didn't know…"

"How could you know, Abby. I never mentioned it."

"…How long is he gone?"

"About two years."

"Again, I'm so sorry."

"Thank you. Please don't mention it in the court house. I really don't want anybody to know."

"I won't. I promise. I know that we are special friends."

"Thank you, Abby," Sarah replied after another short pause. "Maybe you and I can go out one night and talk, just the two of us?"

"I would like that, Sarah. Let's do that. Maybe tomorrow?"

"Well, I don't know about tomorrow. But maybe next week."

"Okay, great! I look forward to it."

xxxxxxxxxx

Abby found Frankie in his usual seat at the bar, one seat from the corner. The corner seat was waiting for Abby.

"Hi Abby," Frankie said as he stood up and pulled the stool out, just enough that the effort was noticed. He seemed to follow Abby with his eyes from her entrance to the empty corner seat.

"Hi, Frankie. Have you been here long?"

"No, just got here." It was the same answer to the same question at every meeting.

"Please have a seat, Abby. What can I get you to drink tonight? Pinot Grigio?"

"No, not tonight. What are you drinking?"

"Dirty martini. Why, you want one of these?" He held his half full glass to eye level as he asked.

"Yes, I want one of those."

"Okay. Can I get one of these for the lady, please. And I'll take another one too. Thanks."

"Thank you, Frankie."

"You're welcome. I'm hoping this means we're gonna have a nice night tonight, Abby."

Abby smiled and gently stroked Frankie's arm. "You never know," she whispered.

Frankie shot Abby a look of muted delight. Then he smiled and touched the top of Abby's hand with his right hand. His left hand almost simultaneously reached down to stroke the inside of her bare thigh.

"Hey, Frankie."

"Hi Andrew. I didn't know you came here."

"Yea, I live right around the corner. I'm here all the time."

"Andrew, meet Abby. Abby, I work with Andrew. He's fairly new but he's getting the hang of things. He's got a great line of shit; talk anybody into anything."

Frankie turned to the bartender and pointed to Andrew's drink, "his drink is on me."

"Hi Abby, nice to meet you. Thanks, Frankie."

"Nice to meet you, Andrew," Abby replied.

"We were just gonna grab a table, Andrew," Frankie said, sliding one of the green olives off the plastic sword in his drink and into his mouth.

"I was just gonna order something myself, food's great here."

"We can eat at the bar tonight, if you like, Frankie."

"You sure, Abby? You don't mind?"

"No, it's fine. We can keep your friend company," Abby said with a smile.

"Great! Thanks, Abby," Andrew exclaimed. "Frankie is my hero. As you might expect, I learn a lot from him."

Abby couldn't keep her eyes off of Andrew. He was tall and thin with wavy brown hair, which looked almost black. His piercing blue eyes seemed to look right through her, but his warm, inviting smile made it seem all right.

He wore a dark colored dress shirt that lay outside of his faded blue jeans. Andrew's jeans were tight fitting and they barely fit over the top of his black boots.

Frankie is watching me look at Andrew, I've got to re-focus…or do I? Abby's thoughts seemed to her to be conspicuous. She gazed at the ceiling for a moment, then she excused herself to visit the ladies room.

"I ordered a couple of appetizers while you were gone."

"That's fine, Frankie. Would you get me another drink, too?"

"Sure. The same thing?"

"Yes, please. It's been a while since I had a martini. I forgot how good they are."

"They are good, Abby," Andrew interrupted. "They go down easy, that's for sure." Abby gladly turned back to Andy and smiled.

The bartender returned with a large shaker and filled all three empty martini glasses to the very top. While Abby was carefully bringing her glass to her mouth, Frankie made a toast.

"To new friends," he said as he turned first to Abby, to his left and then to Andy, who sat to his right.

"To new friends," Abby repeated.

"Yes, to new friends," Andrew said, raising his glass high. Abby noticed that his eyes did not leave her. She didn't mind. She felt a rush of warmth flow through her body, from the top of her head to the bottom of her feet. She tried to ignore the fact that her face felt flushed, and that tingle was back.

The last gulp of martini followed the last bite of the delicious appetizers. Abby was feeling a level of euphoria to which she was not accustomed. She loved it.

"Let's go back to my place for a night cap. I'm right around the corner from here. Whata you say guys, a night cap at my place?"

Abby stood up with more grace than two martinis typically allow. Frankie looked at Andrew, but Andrew only looked at Abby. "Okay sounds good, Abby."

"Yes, it sure does," Andrew agreed.

"Let me grab the check and then we can go," Frankie said as he motioned the bartender.

Abby lead the two gentlemen out of Jesse's and on to the darkened Brooklyn street. "This way, guys. You know the way, Frankie. We'll just follow you." She grabbed Andrew's arm, then Frankie's, while still looking up at Andrew's eyes, and followed Frankie's lead to her house.

During the short stroll to her home, Abby thought back to a discussion she and Frankie had during a recent dinner date. It was the idea of bringing a second man into the bedroom. She forgot, for the moment, who first brought it up, but that didn't much matter. It was clear that they both loved the idea, for different reasons, but they were definitely on the same page.

Once at Abby's house, talk of a nightcap never arose. As soon as they entered the small foyer, Frankie grabbed Abby by the shoulders and spun her around toward him. He kissed her long and hard. She had only gone out with Frankie a few times and it had been a while since she had been with him, but this was a kiss of familiarity.

Abby's knees grew weak, her back arched and her shoulders collapsed into Frankie's hands. Andrew just stood by watching and waiting.

Barely able to speak, Abby whispered to Andrew, without looking at him, "there's a bottle of Dom in the fridge in the kitchen. Grab it, will you, please."

Andrew looked at Frankie and Frankie pointed to the kitchen. "Take me upstairs, Mr. Frank."

"Meet us upstairs, Andrew," Frankie said, not quite at a shout.

"Ok, I'll be right up."

Frankie took Abby's hand and led her upstairs to her bedroom.

xxxxxxxxx

She began to feel the untying of her hands and ankles. Then she removed her blindfold to find the two men walking out of her bedroom without a word.

The room was dark except for the dim moonlight seeping through the white sheer drapes and the hall light that entered through the half opened bedroom door. She lied in the bed for a few minutes, replaying the evening's activities in her mind. She was tired now, very tired.

"What the hell," she heard herself say out loud. She sat back down on the bed. "This whole thing was a set up. They set me up."

She remembered Andrew's comment in the bedroom after she removed her skirt and blouse, 'you were right', he said. It passed over her because of the moment but it was all she could think about now in the solitude of her darkened bedroom.

What's next, she wondered, while stepping into the hot shower. I guess I'll find out soon enough.

xxxxxxxxx

To carry the $100,000 cash, Abby was going to need a bigger bag than she had thought. It had to big enough so it could be rolled up at the top; more secure and easy to handle. She would have to find a bigger bag.

She made the bag fit into her large pocketbook and started out for her appointment. She was running a few minutes late. "He'll wait for me this morning. You can bet on that," she commented to herself as she turned to lock her front door.

In her mind the negotiations were not completed. She envisioned herself giving David half now and the rest when the endorsement was secured. Consequently, she made sure to separate the cash in two very tightly wrapped bundles. "He'll take the $50,000 when it's sitting right in front of him," she said, convincingly.

Her mind wandered as she walked the Brooklyn streets under the overcast, morning sky. She was thinking of a time, recently, when she sat across from her friend and therapist, Dr. Warshak, Hope Warshak.

She had known Hope for some time, probably 10 years or so. She was recommended to Abby by her mom. Her mom said she had sensed some confusion and lack of focus in her daughter during recent visits to the condo.

Hope's husband had worked with her mom so he set up the first meeting. Since that meeting some 10 years ago, Hope and Abby have become close. More than a therapist to Abby, Hope was her friend and confidant.

"So, your friend's name is Sarah? How did you and Sarah become friendly," asked Hope.

'She's an intern from Brooklyn Law School, but she has a background in psychology."

"She does? And, you find that comforting? Do you discuss things with her?"

"Well, yes and I ask her opinion on things that happen."

"This is your second or third new friend since your mother died. Are you aware of that?"

"Yes, I guess so. If you say so. I haven't really been counting."

"I have, Abby. And all of them you have taken into your confidence on some level. Maybe you can arrange to bring Sarah to a session with you one day? You know, just so I can meet her."

"No, she would never come. I could never convince her to come here to see you."

"Try. She might see the importance of the visit since she has a 'psychological background' as you say."

"Okay, I'll try, but I don't think she'll agree to come."

Abby rubbed her hands together in vigorous fashion and looked up at the ceiling. She continued.

"Can we end now? I'm feeling a little anxious."

"Of course, Abby. Do you need another refill?"

"No, I'm good. Thanks very much, anyway."

Abby got up from the chair and started for the door.

"Goodbye, Hope. See you next week," she said without looking back.

"Goodbye, Abby. Have a good week. Give Sarah my regards." Abby nodded.

"Okay," she said.

xxxxxxxxxx

Abby reached David's door. She hesitated for a moment, opened it and entered the foyer to his office.

"Hi, Abby. Come right in," David said through his open office door. There was no assistant here today. Abby fully expected that to be the case this morning.

"Hello, David. Thank you. May I sit down?"

"Please," David said as he indicated with his eyes the chair on which Abby should sit.

Abby followed David's suggestion and sat in one of the two brown cloth-covered armchairs that sat across the desk from him.

David's office looked like it was only a temporary accommodation. Many unopened boxes lay about, and there was nothing hanging on the walls. A few irrelevant knick-knacks cluttered the small shelf behind David's desk.

Knowing they would be alone today, Abby was sure to wear a skirt. David took notice when Abby crossed her legs, but said nothing.

"How can I help you this morning?"

"I have the 'donation' that we spoke about," she said as she held a bundle in each hand. "I will give you 50 now and 50 when I get the endorsement." She lifted each hand, first one then the other, to drive home her point.

"That wasn't the deal, Abby. If a trust issue exists, then you shouldn't even be here."

Abby leaned back in her chair. She uncrossed her legs and put both bundles in her lap. She leaned back slightly more and looked up at the ceiling.

After more than a few moments, she used the arms of the chair to bring her body forward.

"You're damn right it's a trust issue!"

She then leaned in and whispered, "You'll get the other 50 when I get the endorsement!"

"Okay, Abby. If that's the way you want it. I guess I have to trust you, then. We will talk soon."

David watched Abby saunter out of his office. He didn't touch the money until she closed the door behind her.

xxxxxxxxxx

Abby spent the next two or three weeks working hard and waiting for word from either Frankie or David. She found it ironic that two men from opposite ends of the spectrum, in almost every way, had one of the most highly respected judges on the New York State Supreme Court sweating. *Maybe not so opposite*, she thought.

Abby was always in control in her life until she wasn't. And that was a choice that she always made. She always gave up as little or as much control as she desired. She made the rules. This was different.

She spent her evenings in. She felt that she needed to lie low for a while. She spent the time going through some belongings of her mother's, something that she had put off for a little while. Putting it off meant delaying difficult decisions. Procrastination was not typically one of her traits, so she decided to slowly begin the task.

Walter was heard from often, and just as often she turned him down. She needed to sort some things out before she could think about seeing him again.

It was a Saturday, a night that Abby was rarely home. She came across a photo among her mother's things. It was with a stack of other photos.

She sat cross-legged on the carpeted floor of the small room that contained all of her mother's things. Abby was careful to label all of the boxes. So, when she got to the box marked 'photos', she sat down on the floor.

After putting the photos aside from which she was unable to identify anyone, she saved in another pile, those on which the people or places were recognizable to her. One photo in the latter group caught her attention. She stopped before she went on.

"That's my mom and dad and me but who's that other guy?" She spoke softly as if she didn't want anyone else to hear it.

"The guy looks somewhat familiar. Who is it?"

She studied the photo while leaning over in her cross-legged position. She suddenly realized that she could not ask her mother. "The guy looks a bit like a much younger, Walter. Could it be him? It looks like we're going fishing somewhere. Look at me. I can't be more than 10 or 12 there."

Abby leaned back and continued the conversation with herself. "Walter was friends with my dad." She paused. "But, I don't remember him going fishing with us."

She put the picture down on the floor in no particular place. "I'm tired," she said a bit more loudly, as if she was speaking to someone else. I'm goin' to bed."

xxxxxxxxxx

"Sarah, can you please come in here."

"Yes, Judge. I will be right in."

Abby had been debating with herself as to whether she should tell her new confidant about some recent developments in her life. The debate was now over.

"Have a seat, Sarah."

"Thank you, Judge. Is everything okay?"

"Yes. I just wanted to fill you in. I met again with David Jenkins from the conservative party," Abby whispered.

"Oh, you did? Anything come of it?"

"I'm not sure. I sure hope so. I offered to give him $50,000 cash for the endorsement and he demanded 100."

"Really? Did you give it to him?"

"Yes. I had no choice. I want another fourteen years." "I understand, Judge, but can you trust him?"

"I have to. He's taking a bit of a risk, too."

"Well, yes. Maybe. But not nearly the risk that you're taking." "I know and there's more. It seems that I may have been photographed in a compromising situation. I did not follow your advice and I'm sure that it's going to result in me having to pay even more to make sure these photos don't wind up in the wrong hands."

"Do you want to tell me about it, Judge?"

"Not really," Abby shot back. "Not now," she said with a much kinder tone.

"Okay. Well, you know that I'm here if you ever do."

"How 'bout tonight, Sarah, after work? We can go out for a glass of wine somewhere."

"Okay."

"On second thought, maybe you should come back to my place. It'll be more private than a bar."

"Okay, no problem. I will walk home with you tonight."

Abby also realized as she was talking to Sarah that it might be better if Sarah was able to observe the 'scene of the crime.'

"Okay, see you later then, Sarah."

"Thank goodness that Sarah is not an 'I told you so,' kind of person," Abby said out loud after Sarah was out of her office. She smiled but she wasn't sure why.

"Have you ever been to my house?"

"No, Judge, I haven't."

"Well, then, it's about time that you see where I live. Isn't it? And don't call me Judge tonight."

Abby reached for Sarah's arm and led her down the Brooklyn street to her home.

CHAPTER 6

Phillip sat staring straight into his half full glass of beer. The head was gone; it lay flat in the glass. He was thinking about nothing and everything.

"Hi Phil," Frankie said quietly as he approached Phillip at the bar.

"Phillip, please," Phillip said.

"Okay, Phil. I got the photos you wanted."

"I assumed you had them. Otherwise, you wouldn't have called this meeting. Let me see them."

"In a minute. You got the money?"

"Of course. I got the twenty, right here." Phillip patted his jacket on the left breast pocket with his right hand. "I'm afraid twenty won't do it. I need 100 now."

"I can't pay that! It was all I could do to put this together."

"And I almost forgot. There might be some stuff coming down the pike that you and your black robe are gonna have to help me with. I expect you won't have a problem with that, right?"

Phillip leaned back to his left, away from Frankie. "What kind of stuff?"

"Nothin' too big, don't worry"

"That wasn't the deal, Frankie."

"New deal," Frankie said quietly as he took another sip of his JW Blue. "You gotta pay for what you want."

Phillip and Frankie grew up in the same Bronx neighborhood. They hadn't seen each other for years, until recently, that is. They met again at a local casino on a rural Indian reservation. They grabbed a drink and talked about old times and things progressed from there.

Frankie was always the kind of guy who could get things done. Phillip knew that and he also knew enough not to trust Frankie completely.

"Excuse me, Frankie, but I don't think that you have any proof. It'll be your word against mine and I have a pretty good reputation out there. Who's going to believe you?"

"Yea, I guess you're right, Phil. I never thought of that."

Phillip took another sip of his beer. *I just outsmarted a wise guy,* he thought.

Frankie turned to his scotch and silently brought the glass to his mouth. He looked straight ahead as if carefully planning his next move.

"By the way, Phil, did I introduce you to my friend, Andrew. He had the pleasure of meeting your boss, Judge Polk, recently."

"Hello, Phillip. It's nice to meet you," Andrew said from the barstool on Phillip's left side.

Phillip's mouth agape, he shook Andrew's extended hand. "Nice to meet you, too," he said.

"I thoroughly enjoyed meeting the good judge a couple of weeks ago."

Phillip paused, then finished his beer and ordered another. "I guess I have no choice. I don't know how I'm going to do it but..."

"Oh, you'll do it. I'm sure of that," Frankie responded, turning back to his drink. "Now, gimme the twenty you got and get out of here. I'll see you next month same time, same place. Don't let me down, Phil."

Phillip took a large gulp of his fresh beer, and without a word, put the envelope on the bar and walked out.

We'll take two more," Frankie said to the bartender while placing the envelope in his jacket pocket. Andrew moved onto the barstool that was vacated by Phillip.

After a few minutes, Phillip reappeared. "What about the pictures," he said, timidly.

"In two months, after the third payment. I need half before I even think about turning them over to you." Phillip again exited in silence.

"Now it's time to put a call into her honor, don't you think, Andrew."

Andrew just shook his head and smiled.

Frankie was well respected by Andrew and everyone with whom they worked. He had a reputation for eloquence and charm. He had the innate ability to convince both men and women of most anything; men in 'business' and women for other purposes in order to suit his needs.

"I'll go see her when the time is right."

"Okay, Frankie." Andrew paused briefly then asked, quietly "any reason we can't squeeze 'em both?"

"No reason, I see. I like the way you think, kid."

xxxxxxxxxx

"Walter is on the phone, Judge."

"Okay, thanks, Lisa. I'll take it."

"Hello, Walter. How are you?"

"I'm fine, Abby. How are you? Been tough getting a hold of you."

"I'm sorry, I've just been so busy lately."

"Well, do you have any more time now?"

"Yes. What did you have in mind?"

"Anything. I just want to see you."

"Okay. How about dinner at my place on Saturday night? Most people consider my cooking to be acceptable." Abby offered a short giggle.

"Okay, sounds good. I'll give you my opinion as a gourmet." They both chuckled at Walter's comment.

"About 6:00 then," Abby finally said.

"That'll be fine. I'll bring the wine."

"Great, see you then."

"Yes, see you then. Text me your address when you get a chance."

"Of course. Goodbye."

"Bye, Abby."

xxxxxxxxxx

"Phillip, will you please come in here. Thank you." "Yes, Judge. I'll be right in."

Abby turned to Sarah, who was seated on the sofa and said, "I'm glad you're here to hear this. Just listen and tell me your reaction after Phillip leaves."

"Have a seat, Phillip. I'll get right to the point, Phillip. You seem to be a bit distracted lately. Is everything alright?"

"I'm good." Phillip could not hide the surprise in his voice.

"I know that gearing up for a campaign can be time consuming, but please try to stay focused on the work we have here. I feel like we are falling behind on some of this motion work."

"No, I think we are pretty much up to date."

"I hope so."

"Yes, Judge,"

"Thank you, Phillip."

Sarah sat quietly with her pad and pen in hand. Abby watched Philip leave her office.

"Is there anything going on out there that I should know about?" The Judge turned to Sarah as she settled into the same chair that Phillip just vacated.

"No, Judge, not that I can see."

Abby leaned back in her high-backed chair and stared at the ceiling above her desk for what seemed like a long time to Sarah.

Leaning forward, Abby whispered, "I think Phillip and Lisa are having an affair. I've thought so for some time."

"Really, Judge. What makes you say that?"

"Just some things I've seen. Keep your eyes open. They're both married," Abby paused, "it's a scandal that nobody needs now." She leaned back in her chair again.

"Of course, it would be worse for him than for me."

"That's true, Judge. The timing would be bad for him, to say the least."

"Yes, it would, wouldn't it? Just keep your eyes open, please. Thank you, Sarah."

xxxxxxxxxx

Abby liked to cook. It was one of her favorite ways to pass the time. She found it therapeutic. It relaxed her. Her dishes were passable and that was good enough for her.

She was planning on serving roasted chicken at her intimate, Saturday night dinner. She knew that the menu was not as important as the explanation that she knew she owed to Walter.

Walter arrived right on time with flowers in one hand and a bottle of an Italian red in the other. It had been some time since Abby had last received flowers from anyone.

"Thank you, Walter. This is very nice," Abby said through a broad smile at the door. She looked down at the cellophane wrapped bouquet.

"Come in, won't you please, Walter."

"Thanks, Abby."

"Make yourself comfortable, while I find a vase for these beautiful flowers."

"Okay." Walter sat on the cocoa brown leather couch.

He wore a medium gray sports coat, an open collared white shirt, and pair a black dress slacks. She remembered he seemed a bit uncomfortable in a suit and tie at the Judge's Dinner

"Can I get you a glass of wine?"

"I'm good for right now. I'll have some wine with dinner though."

"I have soda or juice and of course water also."

"Maybe a glass of cold water, please. That would be great."

"Cold water, right. Coming up."

"I'll have some water, too," Abby said, as she sat down next to Walter on the couch.

"Cheers. To us," Walter said through a warm smile.

"Cheers," Abby replied, above the sound of the clinking glasses. Abby took pause. She took a sip of the cool water and leaned back on the soft couch.

"Maybe we should talk," she finally said. "I think I owe you an explanation." She paused again. "You know, for my behavior the last time we were together."

"Only if you feel like you need to, Abby. I ask for nothin'," Walter replied.

"Thank you, but I want to explain. It was the baby-girl comment. My father used to call me his little baby-girl. It just hit me wrong. Sorry."

"I didn't know…"

"…How could you?"

"I'm sorry that I hit a nerve…"

"Not a nerve, a good memory actually… I just want to keep that memory between me and my dad, if you don't mind, Walter."

"No worries. I get it. I'll lose the baby-girl."

Abby leaned over and kissed Walter on the cheek. "Thank you," she whispered. "Thank you for understanding."

"Now let's have that glass of wine," Walter said softly.

"I have something even better for our toast. How about a glass of champagne?"

"Sounds great! You need help?"

"No, I don't think so," Abby responded as she opened the small wine fridge under the counter. "I got it."

Walter watched Abby while she held the bottle away from her body and over the sink while struggling to remove the cork.

"Are you sure you don't need a hand?"

Just as Abby was going to answer him, a loud pop came from the tightly held bottle followed immediately with an eruption of its foamy contents.

"Oh," Abby exclaimed.

"Yes, maybe you can grab a couple of these glasses here on the counter."

Walter took the bottle from Abby and stopped the flowing champagne. He poured the wine into the glasses over the sink and wiped the bottle before placing it in the ice bucket which sat on the counter.

Abby wiped her hands and smiled. "Thanks for coming to my rescue. I probably would have lost it all down the drain."

"That's why I'm here, Abby." Then he leaned over and kissed Abby on the cheek. "Let's have that toast."

"To new beginnings," Abby said, holding her glass up.

"Yes, to new beginnings," Walter repeated. He reached over and very softly kissed Abby on her lips. She closed her eyes and silently begged for more. She got it.

Walter gave Abby a long loving kiss. Abby's knees got weak. It was like nothing she had ever experienced prior. She wanted more.

"Let's grab the bottle and go sit inside," Walter said. He had been around long enough to know that a slower pace was important, especially with this lady. There was a lot of stuff in this woman that needed to come out slowly, very slowly.

xxxxxxxxxx

"I think I could fall in love with this man, Hope."

"Really, Abby? I think, that's the first time I ever heard you say anything like that. It's nice to hear. Tell me about this man that has turned your head?"

"His name is Walter. He's an old friend of my father's. They used to work together in the courthouse. They were both clerks back in the day."

"A friend of your father's, you say? Where did you meet him?"

"I met him at my 'Judge of the Year' affair, a few months ago. He treats me like a lady. It's wonderful."

"I've never seen you like this, Abby. You're giddy. I'm happy for you. Just be careful. Make sure that the feelings that you are beginning to have for this man don't come from your longing for your father."

"They don't," Abby answered abruptly. "I don't need you to put a negative spin on this." Abby couldn't look at Hope after she responded.

"That's not what I'm trying to do, Abby. I just want you to be aware of your feelings. I don't want you to get hurt. That's all."

Abby didn't answer. She looked past Hope at the wall which displayed her diplomas in neat alignment.

When Abby met with Hope, they sat across from each other in high-backed, beautifully upholstered chairs. They sat about 4 feet apart with nothing between them. Hope held a pad and pen and Abby sat mostly with her hands clasped in her lap.

This conversation had Abby with her arms closer to her body- on the arms of the chair. She hunched over a bit and locked her ankles together.

"I don't like coming here and being attacked by you. I think I'm going to cut this session short. I'll see you next week."

"Okay, Abby," Hope said to Abby's back. "See you next week."

Abby stopped after taking only a few steps in the hallway outside Hope's office door. The tears just began to flow. She didn't try to stop them; she just let it happen. She leaned against the wall with her face in her hands and sobbed. It felt good. She wasn't exactly sure why she was crying, only that it was having a cleansing affect.

"Abby, why don't you come back in and we can talk about this." Hope's words were soothing. She put her arm around Abby and led her back into her office and to the beautifully upholstered armchair.

Abby sat with her head bowed sniffling into a tissue that she retrieved from the box on the table next to her chair. She was sure that she would not have allowed Hope to restart the session had she not had her hallway cry. She felt like talking a bit now.

"Do you feel like talking about your dad, Abby? It might be time again."

The tissue partially covering her face, Abby nodded.

"You had a very good relationship with your dad, right?"

"Yes," Abby whispered, barely looking up.

"And you were upset when you found him, right?"

Abby nodded again. She said nothing. Her quiet sobbing increased. She reached for another tissue.

"But you also felt confused and alone, didn't you?" "He was my whole world."

Hope nodded. "You looked up to him with love and adoration. You loved him very much."

"I did," Abby sobbed.

"I know, dear. It's alright."

"And scared. I was very scared." She looked up at Hope and spoke clearly through the tears.

"That's understandable for anyone, but especially a young girl."

"I felt like I didn't have anyone. My mom, yes, but she was going through her own stuff after Dad died. A sister,I always wished that I had a sister." Abby sat up a little straighter and reached for another tissue, her crying having subsided to some degree.

"And the reason. I always asked myself why. Why did he do it? Why did he kill himself?"

Abby was looking directly into Hope's eyes now, but Hope didn't have the answer. Abby looked away. For that moment only the tissue provided comfort.

"We'll never know. Nobody will ever know," Abby said softly into that tissue.

Hope sat quietly for a few moments, then she said, "no, probably not, Abby."

"For years I thought it was something I did. Maybe I disappointed him somehow."

"It wasn't you…"

"I know that now, but I didn't then."

Abby didn't like it when Hope talked to her as if she was a child. *She could be* so *condescending*.

The two woman sat silently for a few minutes. Hope was looking at Abby and Abby sat with her hands, again, clasped in her lap, looking past Hope.

"Why would you have wanted a sister, Abby? So, you could confide in her? Do you think that would have made you feel less alone and afraid?"

"A sister is your best friend, isn't she? Yes, somebody to talk to."

"You couldn't talk to your mom? What about friends? Did you have any friends?"

"Yes, I had many friends, but never for very long. My mother shut things down for a while after my dad died; no more after school activities and very few of my friends were allowed at the house. My mother never wanted people around and she didn't want to talk to me very much. I spent most of my time, alone, in my room."

Abby leaned back and looked at the ceiling for a few moments, before continuing. Hope looked up from her note pad.

"Who knows, maybe she blamed me for my dad's death," Abby said softly while returning her gaze from the ceiling tiles. "I am the one who found him. We didn't talk about it much."

"Maybe she blamed herself," Hope said softly, her eyes focused on Abby's face.

Abby sat quietly with her hands clasped together in her lap.

"Maybe," she finally said.

"Maybe your mom was feeling some of the same things that you were feeling after your dad passed away."

"I thought of that, but I dismissed it. I guess I was being a little selfish. I was only thinking of myself and what I was going through."

Abby pointed her gaze at the ceiling again. Hope sat quietly. She held her pen with both hands over her pad, which sat idly in her lap.

Hope was a tall, thin woman. She wore glasses and her light brown hair was seemingly always wrapped up in a bun on the back of her head.

She usually wore dark colored pantsuits and dark shoes without a heel. She didn't feel the need to be any taller.

Abby thought that Hope's large, round, black-rimmed glasses were too big for her face, but of course, she never said anything. Sometimes Hope would take them off her head and lightly chew on the end while Abby spoke.

Abby couldn't help but notice that Hope was significantly more attractive when her glasses were in her hands. Abby noticed something else about Hope; she rarely, if ever, smiled.

"Many times, if I saw that my mom looked sad, I would ask if she was alright," Abby continued. "She always answered, 'yes, I'm fine' and go on with what she was doing. I finally stopped asking."

"Some people keep everything in. That sounds like your mom. Unfortunately, that probably didn't benefit either one of you during the grieving process, especially you, at your young age. I'm sure she did the best she could though, Abby."

"I needed to talk to someone, Hope," Abby said through fresh tears. "I needed her then."

"I know, Abby," Hope said as she leaned in with a new tissue. "I know."

CHAPTER 7

"Judge, Walter is on the phone."

"Thank you, Phillip. Where's Lisa?" Abby had just made herself comfortable at her oversized desk.

"I believe she's still on her lunch break."

"You guys didn't go to lunch together today?"

"Not every day, Judge."

"Oh, my mistake, Phillip... Hello, Walter. How are you?"

"Great, Abby. Is this a good time?"

"Yes, it's fine. I'm alone."

Phillip stopped at the door and shot the judge a look before he closed the door behind him. Abby's brief satisfaction was reflected in her short smile.

"Walter, did I tell you that I think my law man and my secretary are having an affair."

"No, Abby. Are you sure? Both are married, aren't they? Oh well it's been known to happen. Hope it doesn't get out, for the sake of his judgeship and all.

"I'm not talking about it to anyone but you. I don't spread gossip. But you and I are getting so close, I just figured ..."

"...Okay, just be careful. We can talk more about it later. I'm seeing you later, right?"

"Yes, I'll meet you after work at the new Italian restaurant that we talked about. The one near my house."

"Okay, great, see you about 6:00."

"Alright, then, see you later."

"Bye, Abby."

"Good bye, Walter. Love you."

"'Love you!' Where the hell did that come from?"

Abby arrived at the restaurant that evening to find the line of patrons to be seated spilling out on the Brooklyn sidewalk. Making his way out of the front entrance of Maestro's was Walter.

"Honey, they say it's a two hour wait. Wanna go over to Jesse's instead?"

"Really, two hours?"

"Yea. It's very small inside. It smells great in there though. We gotta come back another night. C'mon, let's go over to Jesse's. It's right around the corner."

"Okay," Abby hesitated before she agreed.

Abby studied the bar quickly as soon as they entered Jesse's. *All good!*

"There's a wait for a table here, too. You wanna eat at the bar?" Walter asked while perusing the bar. "There's a couple of seats over there in the corner. Those people are getting up. C'mon let's grab 'em."

Before Abby could answer she was led by the hand to the corner of the bar.

"You guys leaving?" Walter asked with a smile. "Yes," one of the strangers responded.

"Thanks," Walter said, still smiling.

"They didn't look very happy," Walter commented to Abby when the couple was out of earshot.

"Maybe they were fighting."

"Maybe. What can I get you to drink, Abby?"

"Just a glass of Pinot Grigio, please." Abby sat on the corner barstool with her eyes still searching.

"Two Pinot Grigios and a couple of menus, please." The bartender reached for the menus right away. He put them down on the bar and shot a quick acknowledgement to Abby.

With Abby's back against the wall, her eyes kept busy. "Cheers! To good health and old/new friends," Walter proclaimed.

After a sip of wine or two, Abby decided that there was no need to be on guard any longer. She was able to convince herself that even if he did come in *he would be cool.*

"Hello, Abby. What a coincidence running into you here. Didn't know that you came here."

"Hi, um…Frankie right?"

"Yes, Frankie. I ran into our mutual friend, Phillip, not too long ago. Is he still workin' for you?"

"Yes, He's still my lawman… Walter, this is Frankie. Phillip, my lawman, and Frankie are friends." Abby tried not to let it sound like she had just become aware of that connection.

"Hello, Frankie. Nice to meet you," Walter said as he stood to shake Frankie's hand.

"Glad to meet you, Walter. Let me get the next round." Frankie signaled the bartender.

"Thank you, but that's not necessary," Walter said with his eyes on Abby.

"No, please. I insist."

"Okay. If you insist, thanks."

"I'm waiting for a friend so I'm gonna grab those two stools, over there. It's nice to see you again, Abby. Tell Phillip that his old friend, Frankie, says hi, would ya. Thanks."

"He's quite a character, isn't he," Walter said trying to illicit some sort of a response from Abby. Her silence, unbeknownst to her, was deafening.

"Yes, he is," Abby replied, meekly. "Yes, he is."

She couldn't help wondering who Frankie was meeting. *Was it going to be Andrew? And if so, could she keep this up? Would he be as cool? Any other surprises?*

"Have you decided on what you're going to order, dear?"

"No. I haven't even looked at the menu yet. Let's see."

Abby picked up the menu that lay in front of her, but she could not concentrate. The words she read meant nothing. "I'll just have a shrimp cocktail," she said after a short silence.

"That's it. No dinner?"

"No, thank you. I'm not that hungry tonight. Besides the shrimps here are huge."

"Okay. I'm gonna have a steak." Walter smiled. "I'm kinda hungry."

Abby shot a glance toward Frankie just in time to witness him welcome a tall willowy blonde woman to the empty bar stool beside his. *Really? I wonder who she is. What the hell?*

She quickly returned her gaze to Walter who was clearly observing her observations. *Focus, Abby.*

"I bought your friend and his date a drink," Walter said softly. His eyes never left Abby.

"He's not my friend. I…I just know him through Phillip."

"Whoever he is; I bought them a drink."

"Okay. But you didn't have to."

"I know I didn't have to, honey. I wanted to. He bought us a round. One good turn deserves another, ya know."

Abby could only manage a shallow smile in response. Walter's smile lingered awhile.

"Thanks for the drink. We're gonna grab a table inside," Frankie said with his date's arm inside of his.

"Our pleasure," Walter replied.

"Why don't you join us for dinner?"

"I don't know. What do you think, honey? It might be fun," Walter said.

"I don't know," Abby said, only looking up as she spoke.

"C'mon, Abby. It'll be a lotta laughs," Frankie cajoled.

"Okay," Abby finally said, timidly looking at Walter.

"We'll take a couple of bottles of wine," Frankie said to the waiter before the startled server could say a word. "One Pinot Grigio and one Chianti. The best you you've got. Thanks."

"Very good, Sir," the waiter replied before turning away to fulfill the latest request.

"Oh, by the way, this is Stacy. Stacy, this my friend, Abby and her friend, Walter. Abby and I have a friend in common."

"Hi, Stacy," Walter said as he extended his hand. "Hello Stacy," Abby said. They did not shake hands.

Stacy turned out to be okay, but that didn't make Abby feel any more comfortable. Her thoughts were all over the place.

She was sitting having dinner with a man who she had been with recently and who she was sure was very shortly about to blackmail her. She knew that she was as responsible as anyone for what happened that night, and soon she was going to pay, somehow.

Maybe worse than all that was the fact that she was now feeling pangs of jealousy as she sat across from this beautiful, somewhat dignified woman who was obviously into 'her pal, Frankie.' These thoughts, together with the notion that Walter, the guy with whom she really wanted to build something, was definitely suspicious, kept Abby quieter than usual at dinner.

"You okay, Abby," Frankie asked between bites of porterhouse. You've hardly said a word tonight. Is she always this quiet, Walter?"

"Are you all right, honey? You are a bit quiet."

"Yes, I'm fine. Thank you for asking, Walter. Just thinking about a trial that I'm starting on Monday."

"No business talk tonight. I won't hear of it. There'll be plenty of time to talk business later," Frankie said, looking directly at Abby as he poured her some more wine.

Walter shot Frankie a look then he turned back to Abby. Then looking at Frankie, he said. "Not sure what you mean by that, Frank."

"Nothin'. I don't mean nothin'."

"Maybe we should go, Abby."

"Okay," Abby quietly agreed and nodded.

"This should cover it," Walter said as he placed some money on the table. "It was a nice evening. Thanks. It's time to get home now."

"Right. Fun night. Nice to meet you, Walter. I'm sure we'll meet again," Frankie said before he went back to his steak.

xxxxxxxxxx

Abby needed to clear her head. The Sunday morning sun was bright and the sky was clear. There was a chill in the air but it was welcomed. A long walk on this crisp Sunday morning was just what the doctor ordered.

She knew that Frankie was gonna come down on her. If she wasn't sure of it before the other night, it was confirmed at dinner.

Abby stopped at the Promenade, took a seat on one of the benches. *What?* she thought. *What's he going to want?*

The long, cool walk along the east river did the trick. Her head was clearer. It was time to find out. It was time to reach out to him.

Before Abby was able to jump into the shower, her phone rang. "Hello Abby, it's Lisa. Sorry to bother you on the weekend, but I have a problem and I need to talk to someone."

Abby could hear the urgency in Lisa's voice. Lisa was always very calm in the courthouse. There seemed to be no problem that rattled her. Abby was able to entrust her with many issues that arose during the work-day. She did so with the utmost confidence that Lisa would handle each efficiently and expeditiously.

"No bother, Lisa. How can I help? Would you like to stop by and talk?"

"Yes, if I could. I mean, if it's not too much trouble." "No trouble at all. Give me an hour. Do you have my address?"

"No, I don't."

"I'll text it to you. See you in about an hour."

While in the shower, Abby tried to consider what the substance of the upcoming conversation was to be. She spoke softly to herself under the hot running water.

"I don't think Lisa knows that I know about the affair. Heck, I don't think that Phillip knows that I know. What else could be so important that it required a weekend visit?"

When Abby opened the door to welcome Lisa, she could see that Lisa was visibly shaken. Her unmade face was drawn and colorless, and her sunken eyes were swimming in dark circles. She stood timidly, not very close to the door, unsure of her next move or even her next word.

"Come in, Lisa."

"Thank you, Judge."

"Please, call me Abby. Won't you have a seat. Can I get you something to drink, some coffee or juice?"

The kitchen table to which Abby led Lisa was round and only large enough for four. It stood on a brightly colored circular rug. At times, Abby thought that the flowers in the rug might be too big and bright for her kitchen, but the rug almost always elicited a compliment from visitors.

"A cup of coffee if you have it made already; otherwise, a glass of water will be fine."

"I don't have the coffee made, but I will brew some..."

"...No, don't..."

"...It's alright, I could use a cup, too."

"Okay, then. Thank you."

"Please have a seat anywhere at the table. Make yourself comfortable."

"Okay, thanks."

Lisa pulled out a chair and sat facing Abby. Abby readied the percolator. Lisa looked intently at Abby, then she lost focus; she saw nothing, just some meaningless movement.

"What's on your mind today, Lisa?"

"I'm, uh, not sure if you know, but, uh, I've been seeing Philip after work. I don't know how it started…it just started and it's been going on for a while now."

"I had a feeling that something might have been going on, but I wasn't sure."

Abby was careful not to mention the source of the information.

"Well, now I have a big problem. My husband knows."

"How?"

"I don't know, but he knows, and he's livid."

"How can I help?"

"I just wanted someone to know. I'm not sure what he's going to do. I just wanted someone to know." Lisa lowered her head and started to sob quietly.

Abby paused. She was sitting now, in a chair next to Lisa, holding the top of Lisa's left hand.

"Did you try to talk to him?" Abby asked in her most soothing tone.

"I can't talk to him. He's fit to be tied. I'm scared, Abby. I've never seen him like this. I mean I'm really afraid—and not just for me."

"What do you mean?" Abby knew the answer

"I mean, I'm afraid for what he might do to Phillip. He's a big guy…strong too."

Abby hesitated before she asked the next question. "What about his guns?"

"No, He would never. His pistols are all put away in the safe. Besides he doesn't need a gun. He could do plenty of damage just with his two hands. You know how thin Phillip is. He could break him in half and he just might."

The tears stopped and Lisa looked up at Abby as if for some guidance.

"Not much I can say, Lisa. You got yourself into a real situation here. I imagine a visit to Phillip's wife is the very least you can expect from your husband.

"Yes, of course, you're right. I don't know what to do." Lisa began to sob again. Abby was starting to lose her patience.

"You need to go home to your husband and beg his forgiveness, maybe suggest counseling. And you need to tell Phillip that your husband knows and that it's over. Stop thinking about yourself for once. For God's sakes, Lisa, enough is enough!"

Abby returned to the coffee pot to refill her cup.

The sobs were louder and sloppy by now. "You're right, Judge. I'm sorry. Thank you."

"No need to apologize to me. I'm not the person that deserves your apology. Now, go home to your husband. Try to salvage your marriage. Go ahead."

"Okay, I will. Thank you, Judge, Abby

After Lisa left, Abby thought back to the one time that she had met Lisa's husband. Lisa was right; he was a big guy. Abby smiled at that prospect. She then unplugged the coffee pot and picked up her cell phone; her call couldn't wait any longer.

On second thought, maybe it could. She poured herself a glass of sherry and looked out through her dining room window, over the burgeoning Brooklyn streets. Another Sunday in the city.

CHAPTER 8

"Hello, Frankie, it's Phillip."

"I know who it is. You're a little early. I wasn't expecting your call for another couple of days."

"I have it all. I want the photos."

"You have the whole 100?"

"Yes. When can we meet?"

"Meet me at the Promenade in an hour. Text me when you get there."

"Okay."

Phillip arrived with a new brown leather brief case in hand and the voice memos app activated on his phone which sat in his inside breast pocket of his sports jacket. He wasn't sure what he hoped to accomplish but he thought it couldn't hurt.

"Hi, Phil. I assume that's the money. If it is, I gotta say, I like the way you do business. Let me take a look."

Phillip, seated on the bench to the right of Frankie, released his grasp on the briefcase. Frankie opened it slowly, but only partially, to check its contents. Frankie, then, put the briefcase on his left side, never releasing his tight grip on its handle.

He nodded. "I do like the way you do business, Phil."

"Okay, Frankie. What about the pictures."

"Here's the thing, Phil. I don't have them with me. Thought I would start taking bids. Ya know, you and your boss, highest bidder. That kinda thing."

"C'mon, Frankie! Stop playing games. I gave you the money; you didn't have to wait. I want those pictures."

"Couple of things. One, I don't play games when it comes to money and B, don't ever tell me what to do. I make the rules. I always make the rules and you need to remember that." Frankie's tone was barely above a whisper. He then leaned in and said in an even a softer tone, "got that, Phil."

Before Phillip could respond, Frankie reached into Phillip's inside jacket pocket, removed his cell phone and smashed it with his boot heal on the cement below the bench. Frankie then reached down and picked up the largest piece of Phillips broken phone and broke it in half before returning it to Phillip.

"Remember, I make the rules," he said. "Don't call me, I'll call you."

Frankie was man of medium height; about 5ft 10in but he appeared taller. He always wore a dark colored sports jacket, a dark shirt, dark pants and black boots, no matter what the weather.

He wore a gold Rolex on his left wrist and a gold chain on his right. He only wore a pinky ring when he thought he would need to use it. He was well aware of the fact that he commanded attention when he entered a room. He used that when he needed to as well.

His father was a made guy, as was his uncle and grandfather. However, Frankie did not follow in those footsteps right away. His father had wanted a different life for his son.

Frankie tried a few different businesses, some with his 'father's help, and some without. Each provided a different level of success but it wasn't long before the lure of the 'family' business proved to be too much to ignore.

Frankie is smart and it's the kind of smart that the people he wanted to impress, liked and needed. They started him slowly. In the beginning he was assigned mostly collection work.

Frankie was afraid of nothing and that trait carried him well in his new business ventures. His presence commanded attention and his black-eyed stare demanded a response; the correct response.

He was smart enough to know bullshit when he heard it and equipped with a lightning fast right cross to stop its spread. He always got paid, one way or the other.

Frankie was also proficient in the use of martial arts and the small pistol that he always carried on his ankle. He rarely had to make use of either.

Frankie learned early on that fear was a disease and accordingly he was determined to be a carrier. Fear never plagued him. As a result, he controlled every situation.

After a short while, when he had proven to be both trustworthy and efficient, the bosses graduated him to more delicate matters. Frankie earned the reputation of doing what needed to be done. Before long he became an indispensable member of the organization.

Ten years later, almost to the day, he reached the respected status of his father and grandfather. It was in his blood. He never looked back.

Frankie's crew was small, but very effective. His territory was a top moneymaker, year in and year out, and he was not a big spender. Frankie liked to say that he 'flew under the radar'. The bosses noticed and appreciated both his productivity and his self- restraint.

xxxxxxxxxx

Phillip was left looking out onto the East River with pieces of his cell phone in each hand and the remainder at his feet. Let me see, he thought, I received nothing for my $100,000 and I've managed to piss off a wise guy and a burly ex-cop whose wife I couldn't stay away from. "Things are going just as planned," he said softly. He then shoved the pieces of his cell phone in his pocket and started home.

His thoughts immediately went back to that telephone conversation only a few days earlier.

"Hello, Phillip."

"Yes, honey. Hi. I thought we agreed never to call each other after a certain hour. Is everything okay?"

"No, everything is not okay! My husband knows."

"What! How?"

"Does that really matter? He knows! That's all that matters."

"What do we do now, Lisa?"

"We end it. It's done. I have to try to pick up the pieces of my marriage."

"What about, uh…"

"Oh, you mean, what about you, Phillip? I don't know. I know that he is pissed. Keep your eyes open for awhile, and you might consider telling your wife, cause I think she's gonna find out, one way or the other. Up to you."

"You mean, I can't see you anymore?"

"Not outside of work. Yea, that's what I mean, Phillip."

"Okay, Honey. I guess. But I still love you."

"Stop! Just stop! We're done, Phillip. Don't call me again. Don't ever call me again! And no more texts!"

"But, Honey, please, can't we talk about this? I need to see you. Please! I love you."

"Your begging won't work this time, Phillip. It's over."

Phillip's days at work now seemed longer and not nearly as much fun. The light flirting and secret smiles were gone.

"How can you handle this so well?" Phillip whispered his question as he walked briskly by Lisa's desk, a day or two not long after the breakup.

"Phillip, please," was the curt response.

"Yes, Judge. What can I do for you?"

"Yes, Phillip. Thank you for coming in. I noticed that you seem to be off your game the last couple of days. Is everything okay?"

"Yes, Judge. I'm good."

"Listen, Phillip. It's taking entirely too long to decide these motions. I took a stack of the oldest ones to work on myself and we are still behind. Whether or not this is intentional, it has to stop. We need to catch up."

"I assure you, Judge, that it is not intentional."

"I have my doubts. I think that you would like nothing more than to jam me up with the Office of Court Administration. It could serve you well."

"No, Judge, I swear that's not the case."

"Well, then get your head on straight and get caught up. Otherwise I will find another law person. Leave your personal problems at the door when you come to work in the morning."

"Okay, will do. Personal problems, Judge? I have no personal problems."

"I know about your situation with Lisa."

Before Phillip could say a word, Abby cut him off.

"Don't worry, I don't intend to let this get out unless I'm forced to. And you, Phillip, are the only person that can force me."

"That's over now, Judge. She ended it." Phillip decided not to tell Abby the reason Lisa ended it. He thought it would be better that the judge was not aware that her law person was probably a hunted man.

"I thought you two would have ended it during the three month pandemic shut down. We worked mostly from home and I'm sure you didn't see each other as often."

"It just got more intense, Judge; at least it did for me." Phillip realized as that statement left his mouth that it was the first time that he shared anything of a personal nature with his boss, the first time in 14 years.

"Shame on you, Phillip. You have a young wife at home. Don't you want that to work? You need to give that a chance."

"I know. You're right, Judge," Phillip said with a false sincerity in his voice.

Abby thought better than to mention her newly discovered information regarding the connection between Phillip and Frankie. She thought she should save that for another time. It was to be an 'ace up her sleeve'; the first of which that she could remember having.

"Okay, let's get back to work, Phillip," Abby said as she turned her attention to her computer screen. A dismissed and dejected Phillip left the room, looking the part.

Sarah sat quietly on the side sofa observing the goings on. She moved into Phillip's vacant chair upon his exit.

"What do you think Sarah? Was he sincere?"

"Yes, I think he was sincere- as sincere as he is capable of being."

"You have the same impression of him as I do."

"Yes, Abby. We seem to concur often. I noticed that you didn't bring up the Frankie connection."

"I'm saving it."

Sarah didn't respond. She instead looked intently at Abby as if she were waiting for an additional explanation. One did not materialize.

"Well, I better get to work. See you later, Abby. Call me if you need anything more."

Abby did not watch Sarah leave her office. She continued her online legal research. She knew that she needed to get through her pile of motions, as well.

xxxxxxxxxx

Abby picked up her cell phone and looked for Frankie's number. It was time to make the call that she found herself putting off.

"Hello, Frankie. It's Abby. Can we get together for lunch sometime this week?"

"Abby. Hi, Abby. I was just gonna call you. What a coincidence. I'd love to see you. How 'bout Friday at Jesse's?"

"I'd rather not meet there. How about the Tuscan Garden? It's the new Italian restaurant on..."

"I know the place. Perfect!"

"What time is good for you," she asked

"Me? You're the one with the job. What time can you make it?"

"I guess I can be there by 1:00."

"That's great! See you then. Bye, your honor."

Friday came a little quicker than Abby had hoped. In the recent past she had looked forward to seeing Frankie but this time was different. There was, however, a sense of mystery attached to this meeting that made it a bit exciting.

Abby knew that she should be angry. Anger was the first emotion she felt. If and when she did give any time and energy to thinking about that evening her heart would begin to race and her face became flushed. It was a very sensual night, filled with forbidden pleasures.

"I can't think about it", she said to herself as she walked into the restaurant at 12:40 for her 1:00 luncheon appointment.

The restaurant was much smaller than Jesse's. A small bar greeted Abby to the left of the entrance. It barely provided space for 8 solid wooden stools with backs, each medium brown in color. The tables stretched out from there. A row sat along the right wall and one row against the opposite wall, with two rows down the middle.

Before Abby's eyes reached the open kitchen which sat along the back wall, she noticed what looked like a small back room off to the left. The noisy L-shaped restaurant could not have sat more than seventy-five or eighty people. Abby sat at the bar and ordered a ginger-ale from the friendly young bartender.

"I haven't seen you in here before. Is this your first time joining us?" he asked with a fairly heavy Italian accent.

"Yes, this is my first time here. It's very nice. I like the atmosphere. It reminds me of my time in Italy. The restaurants there were so full of life. Everyone always seemed to be having such a good time."

"Yes. It is a simple, how you say, formula; good food, good wine, good people."

"Yes. I guess that's right."

"Are you going to have lunch with us today?"

"Yes, but I'm waiting for someone. I'm a little early."

"Can I get you a glass of wine while you wait?"

"Okay. Maybe a glass of Pinot Grigio."

"Do you like red wine? You must taste this."

Before Abby could respond, the bartender poured a small amount of deep red wine from a large label-less bottle into small stemmed wine glass.

"Try it."

"It's very good. A little sweet, but I like it. It's different from any Italian wine I've had before."

"I knew you would like it," the friendly young bartender said.

"We make it here."

"Really? It's quite good. Thank you."

The bartender smiled, nodded once and filled Abby's glass before he turned to put the bottle away. Abby turned toward the front door as it opened. It was not Frankie.

She turned her head to check the front door at least a dozen more times before she saw Frankie walk in.

"Hi Abby. I hope you haven't been here long. Did Marco take care of you?" Frankie turned to the bartender when he spoke those words.

"Hello, Marco," Frankie said to the smiling bartender. He, then, spoke a few words in Italian to Marco. Marco respectfully responded, also in Italian.

"Ciao, Frankie. Can I get you something," Marco asked.

"No, I think we'll grab a table. Thanks, anyway."

"Everyone seems to know you pretty well here," Abby said quietly as they were being led to their table.

Frankie just smiled and nodded.

Once seated he said, "I own a piece of this place, just a small piece."

"I wasn't aware. You never mentioned it."

"It never came up."

Abby discovered a myriad of different feelings as she sat across from Frankie. She realized that she knew very little about him, only as much as a few dinner dates and fewer still isolated sexual encounters could uncover.

During the lunch more than a few respectful acknowledgements were aimed toward Frankie. They came from employees as well as patrons. Some looked as though they might have been business associates.

What business? She asked herself

"Thank you," Abby said when the waiter poured her a glass from the bottle that had, a moment earlier, been approved by her luncheon date.

"To good friends," Frankie said as he raised his glass.

"To good friends," Abby repeated.

Abby paused as she put her glass down.

"That wine is very nice, Frankie. Thank you. Good choice."

"I'm very familiar with the wine list," Frankie responded with a smile.

"I hope we are good friends, Frankie."

"I think you will find that we are, Judge. Maybe not at first but eventually, I'm sure."

"Frankie's tone was hopeful while at the same time being dismissive.

"I hope so," Abby said. She found herself in a place in which she wasn't comfortable. *A lot rides on those photos,* she thought.

"If you don't mind, I'm gonna order for us." Without waiting for an answer, Frankie signaled for the waiter. "We'll have an order of the cold grilled octopus with the cherry tomatoes, and the fresh fettuccine with the light marinara sauce to split."

The server nodded once and turned away from the table. Frankie took another sip from his oversized red wine glass. Abby watched his every move.

"You and your friend left in quite a hurry from my bedroom a few weeks ago," Abby said as she adjusted the napkin in her lap. It was the first time that she had looked away from Frankie since they sat down.

"We're not gonna talk about that now."

"When?"

"Maybe later."

"When later?"

"When I say so."

The smiles on both sides of the table disappeared. Abby did not look away. She kept focused on Frankie's eyes for a few minutes. Then she silently reached for her glass of wine.

The conversation was, from that moment on, reduced to a very light exchange between two 'friends'. Abby was apprehensive and she didn't hide it well. Frankie was not at all affected with the change in mood. In fact, he seemed to rather relish it.

It wasn't until the two had finished their lunch and were standing outside the restaurant on the sidewalk, that Frankie mentioned anything of substance again.

"We can discuss whatever you have in mind next week if you like. Next Saturday, at Prospect Park say 11:00?"

All Abby could get herself to say was, "Okay, I 'll see you then." Frankie kissed Abby on the cheek and turned to walk away.

"Good friends," he said when he turned back to Abby. "Very good friends."

Abby watched Frankie until he faded into the crowded Brooklyn sidewalk. She was going to have to wait another week. It was going to be a long week.

Sarah was back in the judge's chambers anxiously awaiting the outcome of Abby's meeting with Frankie.

She sat on the small couch in the judge's office with her laptop in her lap, pretending to do research.

"Well," she said, as soon as Abby walked through the office door.

"Not much to report, I'm afraid. We really didn't talk about it much."

"But, I thought that was the purpose of today's lunch." Sarah's words could not hide her disappointment for her friend.

"Yes, that's what I had hoped but, it didn't turn out that way. We have another meeting scheduled for next week. Hopefully we will discuss it in more detail then."

"Next week! You have to wait a whole week? We have to wait a whole week?"

Abby smiled with approval. "Yes, we have to wait a whole week," she said, softly.

"What's happening with the Phillip and Lisa soap opera," Abby asked as she sat down behind her desk.

"Not much. It's been quiet. Maybe your talk with Phillip had its desired effect."

"Let's hope. You'd better get back out there before people start asking questions."

"Okay."

Almost immediately after Sarah left the room Abby received a text from Walter. "Give a call when you can, Abby."

"Hi, Walter. Is everything okay? Are we still on for tonight?"

"Yes, Abby. Of course. I just wanted to know what time you were coming by. I have a nice big porterhouse for two, marinating in my secret sauce. I'm all ready for you."

"I guess about 6:30 if that's good. What can I bring?"

"Nothing, thanks. I have everything we need."

"See you later then."

"I'm looking forward to it."

"So am I."

Abby always felt good after a conversation with Walter, even a short one. He lightened her load with his words. She didn't think he was aware of the effect he had on her.

"I told you not to bring anything," Walter said, when greeting Abby at his front door. "Please, come in, Abby. So good to see you again. You look beautiful as always."

"Thank you, Walter. I just picked up a bottle of wine. I know you like this one."

"Thanks. Let me grab a couple of glasses and we can open this baby, right now. C'mon in, sit down."

"Great!"

"How was your week Abby?" Walter returned to the living room from the kitchen with two freshly filled wine glasses in his hands.

"It was okay. I met with Frankie, today."

"You did. So you decided to take my advice. Great! How did it go?"

"Not much happened. We met for lunch, but we barely talked about it. He said he wanted to wait until next week. We are to meet at Prospect Park next Saturday morning."

Abby paused and looked up at Walter. "He said we will talk about it then," she said, before taking another sip of wine.

"Alright then. He's going to make you wait another week. I'm not surprised. That's how those guys operate."

"What guys?"

"He's got some connections. It's obvious to me. I grew up with some of those guys in the old neighborhood."

"Really? Connections? I guess that's possible."

"It's more than possible, dear. I asked around. Frank is definitely connected. He's known as Frankie The Snake. Some say it's because he can charm anyone out of anything without them knowing it. Others say they call him that for different reasons."

Abby silently took a longer sip of her wine. She looked at Walter with defenseless eyes. "I guess I don't know what I got myself into."

"It's okay," Walter said as he wrapped his arms around Abby.

Moisture filled Abby's eyes as she buried her head into Walter's shoulder. "I didn't know. I didn't know," she said between sobs.

"It'll be okay. You just need to keep me in the loop. I'm here for you."

Abby leaned away from Walter and dried her eyes with his neatly pressed handkerchief. Walter sat back and took a sip of wine. His eyes never left Abby's sad, soulful eyes.

"Ya know, when you told me the story, I must say I was surprised. You played with fire and you got burned. You're a big girl but this is the big leagues here, kid. These guys don't mess around. It's all business with them always!"

Abby nodded. She held the white handkerchief against her nose and mouth. She said nothing.

"Now we have to get you out of this mess. And we will."

Abby nodded her head, again, and whispered, "thank you, Walter."

xxxxxxxxxx

Abby tried to keep her personal feelings regarding Phillip out of chambers but she was finding that to be more and more difficult. She knew she could blow the whistle on the affair but she also knew that she wouldn't. It wasn't her style.

Phillip was not her first choice for law person, or even her second. He was thrust upon her by the local political leaders. They made a backroom deal so she had to live with their choice. But she disliked him from the start and now she was having an increasingly difficult time even being around him.

Phillip could sense Abby's discontentment, but he was either not sharp enough or just too self-centered to sense anything more. There was more, much more and Phillip's weeks became increasingly more difficult.

CHAPTER 9

On Thursday, David called. "It's David Jenkins on the phone for you," Phillip announced upon entering Abby's inner chambers.

Abby smiled. "Thank you," she said, still smiling. "Where's Lisa? Out to lunch?"

"Yes," Phillip said as he walked out of Abby's inner chambers.

"Hello, David. How can I help you?"

"You've got the Conservative Party endorsement. I'll see you in my office this Saturday at 10:00?"

"Thank you, but we have to meet at 9:00. I have an appointment at 11:00."

"Okay. We'll make it 9:00 then. See you then." David hung up before Abby could respond, but that was okay with her. The less she spoke to him the better.

xxxxxxxxxx

"Hello, Frankie, it's Phillip. I've been trying to get a hold of you for weeks now."

"You got me."

"Yea, where have you been?"

"Don't worry 'bout where I've been. You got me now. You're lucky you got me now. You're pissin' me off, Phil. What do ya need?"

"I would like to meet to discuss the way things left off between us."

"You want the pictures. Don't fuck around with me, Phil. I know your game. You want to meet. I'll take a meeting with you, but no pictures."

"Okay. Yes. I want to meet. Where and when?"

"Tomorrow night, 9:30 at Prospect Park, outside the entrance to the zoo."

"9:30? That's pretty late."

"That's it. Take it or leave it."

"I'll take it. See you then. Thanks."

Phillip was not very familiar with Prospect Park or its zoo so he thought he should take a trip down there after work. He needed to check things out before the meeting tomorrow.

His intent was to try to renegotiate with Frankie. If that failed, there was a plan B. Phillip hoped against hope that Frankie would attend the meeting with an open mind.

The next night Phillip stood in front of the entrance of the Prospect Park Zoo for an hour waiting for Frankie.

A winter chill was in the air. Phillip was dressed in an overcoat, scarf and gloves and still was not able to keep warm.

He paced back and forth under the lights surrounding the entrance way, periodically venturing a few steps to either side. He looked out as far as his eyes would take him under the dark moonless sky.

It occurred to him that it must have looked to the occasional passerby or jogger that he was there for a clandestine meeting. He smiled at that thought.

The phone calls and text messages to Frankie went unanswered. So when his watch had indicated that an hour had passed, Phillip decided to go home.

Phillip's home was a modest two bedroom apartment in Brooklyn Heights. It was cold and dark tonight. It was cold and dark every night, he thought, since his wife left.

She said that she just needed time, but he had never seen her so angry...and hurt. He was alone now. No one to talk to and nothing on the stove.

Phillip prepared a cup of tea and a slice of toast and went to bed. No dinner again tonight, he thought. I'll have a big breakfast tomorrow.

Phillip's father was an attorney also. He was well respected for a time. Jake Walsh was a name that everyone in the courthouse recognized.

Phillip and his family lived in a big house on a hill and his father drove his big car to the office everyday, until that is, the truth came out. Pills and alcohol were the cause of Jake's downfall. He lost his family, his practice, and eventually his life to his weaknesses.

Weakness? Maybe it wasn't as much a weakness, Phillip would think sometimes, as a sign of the times. This, coupled with an effort by his father, although misguided, to keep up the lifestyle that and his family had grown accustomed, led to his demise. Phillip had always tried to give his father the benefit of the doubt. It became easier as the years passed.

Phillip's own alcohol demons had caused many problems for him in his younger days. He was thankful everyday that those troubled days were behind him.

His wife was gone, but at least he wasn't drinking again. He closed his eyes to that thought.

Phillip's aging mother was a comfort to him. He spent as much time as he could with her. It was entirely too much time according to his wife but, as she was to discover through recent disclosures, it was not nearly as much time as she was led to believe.

Jake moved out of the family home not long before he died. Phillip was in law school at the time. Having no siblings to help with bills, he decided to get a full time job and continue his education part time. The extra money helped at home.

He rarely thought about his dad. He liked it that way. The brightness of the winter morning brought Phillip little comfort. He was out and off to the courthouse very early that morning. He needed to confront the judge. Rather, he wanted to confront the judge or at least he thought he did.

"Judge, I understand that you were able to obtain the Conservative party's endorsement," Phillip blurted out as soon as the Abby entered his office.

"If you want to speak to me about that, come into my chambers," Abby politely responded, even though no one else was in yet.

Phillip followed the judge into her chamber, but he did not sit when the judge invited him to do so.

"What did you do, tell David about my affair? You bitch."

"No, I didn't. And, Phillip, if you ever call me that again, you will find yourself looking for a job. In fact, maybe once is enough…"

…I have pictures, Judge!"

Abby didn't flinch. She kept a steady gaze on Phillip's angry eyes.

"You do, Phillip? Pictures of what?"

"Pictures of you, that's what!"

Phillip was standing and shouting. He was not comfortable doing either.

"I don't know what you're talking about."

"Yes, you do! I'm a desperate man, Judge. I will do anything to get that endorsement. I have nothing to lose now."

"Okay, Phillip. But we are not talking about this here. Let's meet tomorrow afternoon."

"What time?"

"My last appointment is at 11. How bout 1:00 at my place?"

"Okay, tomorrow at 1."

I'll get the true story at 11, Abby thought as she watched Phillip leave her chambers. I'd better.

Sarah entered Judge's chambers at 9:00 as per usual. "Good Morning, Judge. How are you this morning?"

"Well. Thank you, Sarah."

Sarah sat down. "Everything alright, Judge?"

"Phillip was in here first thing this morning. He said he has the photos. He said he was desperate."

"Do you think he has them?"

"I'm not sure. I don't think so, no. But I'm not sure." Sarah leaned back in her chair never losing sight of Abby's face. "What do you think, Sarah?"

"I think I don't trust him. I don't like him and I don't trust him. That's what I think. Sarah paused. I've got to get to work now. We'll talk later, Judge. Okay?"

Friday night's early spring snow left only a dusting on the park's walkways and grassy areas. The morning sun had made its way through the gray snow clouds and the air was warmer than it had been for the last few days.

Abby had arrived a few minutes early for the 11:00 meeting with Frankie. She stood outside the zoo entrance in Prospect Park as she was directed to do by way of a text she had received the previous day.

She thought of the upcoming meeting. How would it go? Did Phillip really have the pictures?

xxxxxxxxxx

Abby's thoughts turned to a conversation she had with Walter after dinner the night before.

"I agree with you, honey. I don't think that Phillip has the pictures either. I think he was just reaching. Frankie is much too smart to just hand them over to him, at least not until he's put the squeeze on you."

"You think so, Walter? I hope you're right."

Abby looked at her watch. Frankie was late; only 5 minutes but he was late. She started to pace in front of the entrance. It seemed colder now.

"Abby. Let's take a walk."

She turned to see Frankie standing behind her in a long black leather coat and black leather gloves. He didn't look nearly as cold as she was.

"C'mon Judge." Frankie gestured with his head. Abby silently followed. The sun's soothing rays glistened off of the newly fallen snow. The snow was only as deep as a light dusting would provide.

Nothing was said for a few minutes, less time than it felt like to Abby. The silence that even a light snow fall brings to a sunny winter's morning was exacerbated by the wordless stroll.

"As you might have figured, Judge, I have some pictures." "You didn't give them to Phillip," Abby blurted out, anxiously.

"No. Why would I give them to that *Fugaze*."

"Good. Thank you. I suppose you want something from me now, Frankie. I can't pay a lot."

"You're right. I do want something from you." Then nothing. Silence fell between the two, again.

Abby took long, deep breaths as she walked. That seemed to help. Some of her concern had melted away.

"I need you to remember me, Judge, always. You and your black robe, that is. Got me?"

"Yes, I think I do. And, if I do, those pictures will never go anywhere?"

"That's right. They never see the light of day."

"What about Andrew?"

"He already forgot about the whole thing. I made sure of that."

Abby stopped. Then Frankie stopped and turned to look at her. After a brief pause and a few more long, deep breaths, Abby spoke quietly.

"Alright, Frankie, it's a deal."

"I kinda figured you'd see it my way. You got a whole lot to lose, Judge," Frankie said as he turned to continue the stroll.

"And who knows, you might never hear from me again. But, then again, Judge, you might." Frankie smiled and turned to walk back from whence they came. His gaze was straight ahead and unwavering. The judge was left standing and watching.

Abby hesitated for a moment and looked up as if for guidance. She started back only after Frankie was far enough ahead for it to seem that they were no longer together.

Frankie walked, slowly, toward his car which was parked where a 'No Parking' sign stood right outside the front entrance of the park. He always walked slowly but he was walking particularly so, today for a few different reasons. Everything Frankie did was for a specific purpose.

His next appointment was at the Delphi Diner. He requested a sit down with his capo, Benny. They typically met on a regular basis to review finances but this meeting was made outside the schedule, in spite of Benny's seemingly unwillingness to do so.

Frankie arrived first and insisted to be seated at a corner booth. No surprise there; the hostess knew Frankie. He was a regular.

"Thank you, Sweetie," Frankie whispered as he slipped a twenty-dollar bill in her hand. "My friend Benny will be joining me; you know him. Make sure you make him wait a few minutes before you seat him. Be busy when he comes in. Thanks."

Frankie sat facing the door. Benny came in and after a few minutes of waiting, he became frustrated and found Frankie's corner booth on his own. "Hi, Frankie. You wanted to see me."

"Yes, Benny. Hi, I didn't see you come in," Frankie said looking up from his newspaper.

"I'll have a cup of coffee," Benny blurted out to the nearest waiter. Frankie lifted his coffee cup to his lips as if on cue.

Once seated, Benny asked why Frankie requested the meeting.

"First off, I'd like to thank you for taking this meeting with me. Secondly, I just wanted to catch you up on some new developments."

"What are these new developments?"

Before Frankie could answer, Benny's cup of coffee arrived.

"I'll have a couple of scrambled eggs with an English," Benny said to the waiter before he had set the cup on the table.

"Nothing for me; just coffee. Thanks."

"Well?"

"I've been able to get a sitting Supreme Court Justice on the hook. I figured down the road that could be helpful."

"Whaddaya mean on the hook?"

"I mean she owes me. That's what I mean, Benny."

"You know I gotta go back to the boss with this info." Then after a short pause Benny uttered. "Or is that why you mentioned it?"*

"Would you rather I didn't tell you, Benny?"

Benny looked at Frankie and said nothing. His look had clear meaning: 'Frankie, you know that this information will score you points with the boss and you just made me your messenger.'

Before Benny was finished with his eggs, Frankie excused himself to attend another meeting. Benny said nothing.

"I don't want to take any more of your time, Benny. Thanks for the cup of coffee. Can I leave the tip?"

Before Benny could answer, Frankie placed a folded 20 dollar bill under his coffee mug.

"Thanks again."

Benny did not look up from his breakfast.

"Hey, Frankie," Benny said, just loud enough for only Frankie to hear. "You're lucky you're such a good earner; very lucky."

Frankie stopped and turned part of the way toward the booth and smiled. Then he continued on his way.

xxxxxxxxxx

Abby decided to stay at the park after Frankie left. She turned and walked back to where they had just spoken. She stood there and looked ahead, down the walking path.

What was in store for her? Was it all worth it? She remembered a conversation she had with her dad shortly before he passed.

"Cupcake, always remember you're a Polk. You have my name. It's our name. It's a good name. You should be proud of it and never do anything that would tarnish it. You know what tarnish means, honey, right?"

"Yes, Daddy. I know what tarnish means. And I won't do anything to tarnish it. I promise."

"You'll find that, usually, it's pretty easy to tell the difference between right and wrong. Not only do you have to do what's right, but you have to stand up for what's right in certain situations. You need to right a wrong when you can." Then he smiled at his young daughter.

Abby started to walk again, barely able to hold back the tears. *I miss him every day; both him and Mom.*

She reached into her bag for her cell phone. "Dave, it's Abby. I'm sorry I didn't make it to your office this morning. I got tied up. Can you see me now?"

"I'm at the office."

"Be there within the hour."

Abby put her cell phone away and headed for home. He came through so now the final 'donation' was due. She hated to pay him but...

She had recently seen David at a local diner, one that she didn't frequent. He was not alone. He was sitting in a booth, across from a very attractive middle-aged lady. The woman's attire could best be described as casual and alluring. The conversation seemed to Abby to be light and not of a business nature. She remembered when she brought it up to Sarah when she came by Abby's home for the first time. "Maybe you can do some snooping around, Sarah, and find out who that woman is."

"I'll try Abby, but I doubt I will be able to find anything out. By the way, you probably shouldn't discuss things of a sensitive nature in the courthouse. The walls have ears."

"I know. You're right. I thought about that after our last discussion. I should have waited until we met here. Stupid of me." Sarah did not respond. She was pretty sure, however, that she was not going to be able to discover anything regarding David's lady friend. She didn't want to say anything to Abby quite yet, though.

"Whatever we can get on David would be helpful to us. Do what you can."

"I'll look into it, but it could have been anyone, Abby. You know that? Maybe it was his sister."

"I know. I know. I'm just desperate. I wanna save some money."

"I'll do what I can, Judge." Sarah felt like reminding Abby that she thought that the judge was above all this 'snooping'.

"Hello, David." "Hello, Abby."

Despite the failed efforts of the amateur sleuth that was assigned this case, Abby continued on unbridled.

"I saw you at the Grecian Diner a few weeks ago with a very attractive woman."

Dave looked up from his phone. "You did? Ah, why didn't you come over and say hi? I would have introduced you."

"I didn't want to bother you. You looked busy."

"We weren't. Just talking. She's a big fundraiser. Always looking to help out the party any way she can. You shoulda come over." Then an uncomfortable pause ensued. "You don't live near there, to you?"

"No. I was just shopping in the area and I decided to stop for a cup of coffee."

Abby liked the fact that she had to explain herself. It meant that Dave was reeling. *'The best defense is a good offense.'* Abby smiled.

"I have a picture on my cell phone. Where is it? It's here somewhere." Abby scrolled through her phone. "Oh, here it is. I loved your friend's outfit, so I took a quick photo."

"Can we do a little better on the 50,000, Dave," Abby asked softly and very coyly.

Dave leaned back in his high-backed chair and said nothing for a moment. "Yes. I think maybe we can."

"Good. How bout 25." Abby opened the bag and started to count.

"Okay. I guess that's fair."

"Yes, 25,000 for my silence. That's fair." Dave looked at Abby and said nothing.

"Here you go, Dave." Abby placed the neatly bundled cash on the desk and left with the satchel under her arm.

CHAPTER 10

"Hi, Sarah. Are you free to come by for a cup of tea this afternoon?"

"Yes, Judge. What time did you have in mind?"

"Maybe around 4:00. I have some news."

"Okay. That will be fine. See you then."

Abby walked briskly home and placed the satchel under her bed. She would figure out what to do with it later. Now she just needed to lie down. After a brief glance at the clock on her nightstand, she knew she had an hour or so to rest before she needed to get ready for her very small tea party. Sarah would be surprised at the new developments, she thought, as she fell off to sleep.

The doorbell woke her out of a deep sleep. "Oh shit! What time is it?"

She grabbed her robe and ran to the front door.

"I'm so sorry.I fell asleep. Please come in."

Sarah smiled to find the judge in such a condition of disarray. "No worries, Judge. I'll put the water on while you get yourself ready. I brought some tea biscuits."

"Thank you. I will be right down. Let me just throw something on. You've been here before so make yourself comfortable."

Sarah wore her light brown hair in a pony-tail on weekends. She had on faded jeans, a gray sweatshirt which was a size too big, and bright white sneakers.

Her appearance was that of a cute tomboy. She put the water on to boil, the biscuits on a plate, and made herself comfortable on a high stool in the kitchen.

"I saved myself $25,000 today, Sarah. Let's celebrate," Abby, also adorned in jeans and a sweatshirt, said as she entered the kitchen. "Let's break out the champagne."

"That's great, Judge. Congratulations!" Sarah turned off the tea kettle while Abby reached under the counter and pulled out a bottle Veuve Clicquot from the wine fridge.

"Judge, I uh, assume that you haven't heard the news about Phillip?"

Abby was starting to open the orange-labeled bottle. "What news? Did Lisa's husband finally catch up to him?" Abby said with a smile as she went back to her bottle.

"His body washed up on the sand at Coney Island this morning."

"What!" Abby stopped what she was doing.

"Yes. A couple of fishermen found him very early today. I thought you heard."

"No. I hadn't heard. That's terrible. Who would do something like that. I was only kidding about Lisa's husband."

"I know you were. I don't know. I heard he was shot once in the head."

Abby's mind raced to the scene in her childhood basement. She suddenly felt an overwhelming sense of sadness. She felt sadness and sympathy for people she had never met- Phillip's wife and mother. "This is terrible," she said softly.

"Yes, Judge. I know you and Phillip have had your differences but…"

Abby interrupted. "I wouldn't wish this fate on my worst enemy and certainly not Phillip. We worked together for a long time." She sat down at the kitchen island and set the unopened bottle of champagne next to her there.

Sarah came over to Abby and gently rubbed her back. "I'm so sorry, Abby. I really am."

"Thank you, Sarah." Abby's gaze continued straight ahead at nothing in particular.

Just then, Abby picked up her vibrating cell phone. "Hi, Frankie."

"Hi, Abby. I heard about your law man Phil. Too bad. Just wanted to call and give my condolences. If you need anything…"

After a short pause Abby said, "thank you, Frankie. It's just terrible." Neither one said anything for a few moments.

"I have to go now, Frankie. Thanks again for calling." She hung up without waiting for a response.

Abby sat for a few minutes, saying nothing and thinking about Phillip and Frankie and that connection. She thought about her dad and that afternoon after school. She thought about her mom and she even thought about Phillip's dad. She forgot Sarah was there.

Abby then dialed Walter's number. "Phillip is dead."

"Really? How?"

"Can I see you tonight?"

"Yes, of course, sweetie. I'm so sorry to hear about Phillip."

"I'll come by your place maybe about 6:30?"

"That's fine. And again, I'm sorry."

"Are you okay, Abby," Sarah asked.

"I'm not feeling very well right now, Sarah. You'll have to excuse me. I need to lie down." Abby retreated to the sofa in the living area.

Sarah said nothing. Her eyes followed Abby as she walked away. She put the champagne back in the wine fridge.

Sarah watched as Abby sat up on the sofa and started to dial her cell phone again. "I guess I should call Phillip's wife. You know, to extend my condolences."

Sarah nodded her head. "Good idea," she said softly.

"Hello, Diane. It's Abby Polk. I just heard. I'm so sorry. If there's anything I can do..."

"I'll bet you are, Abby. You wanted him dead as much as anyone. Now you have no competition for what you want. You might as well have pulled the trigger."

"In politics it's each man..or woman for himself. You know that, Diane."

"Well if you didn't make so many enemies, none of this would have happened."

"Diane. Diane, are you there?" When no one responded Abby hung up and put her head on the sofa pillow.

When Abby awoke she was alone in her apartment. She did not feel well-rested. She felt very drained today; like she was coming down from some long, drawn out adrenaline rush.

It was time to get ready to go to Walter's place but she couldn't get off the sofa. She couldn't move at all. She closed her eyes for a few more minutes as she tried to motivate herself to get up. She finally did, but she wasn't gonna go to too much trouble. Walter would have to take her pretty much as she was today.

She threw on a pair of jeans, flats, and a button down shirt. Her hair was pulled back and she had on very little makeup when she knocked on Walter's door.

"Hi, Abby. How are you feeling?"

"Not great, Walter. I just can't believe it. Who would do something like this?"

"Come in. Sit down. I'll get you some wine."

"Thank you."

Walter joined Abby on his couch with two glasses of Pinot Noir. He knew it was her favorite red wine. She liked the light-bodied red wines.

"I have some news that you might find interesting," Walter said as he handed Abby a large red wine goblet. "I picked these wine glasses up today. Do you like them? You're makin' me class up the place."

Abby smiled and took a long sip.

"That's not my news," Walter said with a quick smile. "I knew about Phillip. I still have some connections out there." Abby said nothing. "After I talked to you today, I put a call into a buddy of mine. He is retired from the DA's office. He was a detective investigator there for about 15 years."

Abby took another long sip and put her glass down on the coffee table. "Do I know him?"

"I don't think so. His name is Dick Shepard. Do you know him?"

"No, I don't think so. What did he have to say?"

"He said he knew who Phillip was, but only because he knew Phillip's old man, Jake. Jake was a big time lawyer who got jammed up…"

"I know all about it. He got disbarred and spent a year or two in jail."

"Right, but did you know that he had a connection to your father."

Abby looked up. "I knew they knew each other from the court house, but what kind of connection?"

"When the DA's office was trying to put together a case against Jake, your father was scheduled to testify before the grand jury. Your father's untimely death prolonged the investigation against 'Ole Jake' for months. He almost skated."

"What did my father know?"

"It seems that an irate client approached your dad during a break in his courtroom one day and not knowing where else to go, spilled the beans on Jake. Your father tried to direct her to the local bar association but the woman wouldn't take a breath. She just kept talking."

"All they had to do was subpoena the woman. It doesn't explain why my dad was involved."

"Well, your dad being the kind of guy he was, did some digging. You remember, he was very black and white. There was right and wrong and nothing in between."

"Yes, I remember." Abby finished her wine.

"Some more wine?" Walter poured.

Abby held out her glass. "Yes. Thanks."

"Sorry to hit you with this, today. I just thought you might like to know."

"Thank you, Walter. You sure gave me some stuff to think about."

"I can do some snoopin' around if you like."

"Not sure what I want, right now. Let me think about it for awhile. A lot to digest."

"You alright'?" Abby didn't answer right away. Her pensive gaze brought her to her wine glass. She held it front of her facw, turning it slowly, as if searching for an imperfection in the glass.

She put the glass down in front of her. "I think I need to leave now. I need to go home, Walter. I'm sorry."

On the short walk home, Abby's mind raced without focusing on anything in particular for very long. She knew she would have to tell Sarah about this new development as soon as she could!

xxxxxxxxxx

"Why are you calling me for another meeting, Frankie? We just met a few weeks ago." Benny's question was not unexpected.

"I just felt like that meeting could have ended better. I wanna make sure we're good. That's all."

"We're never good, Frankie, you know that." Bennie let out a short laugh, Frankie didn't.

"I wanna try to correct that. So, we'll meet tomorrow at Gino's for lunch. We'll have a little pasta and a little wine outside on the sidewalk. See you then."

"Okay, Frankie. I'll be there. I'll see what you got to say."

"Okay, Benny. Good."

A meeting with the underboss precipitated Frankie's invitation. This meeting was something that was insisted upon. Frankie, as usual, did what he was told.

It was not an ideal day for an outdoor lunch. The sky was overcast and it looked of rain, although none was in the forecast. It was warmer than usual for this time of year. Frankie wondered if the dark skies could be to his advantage.

He arrived early and made sure to be seated at a corner table. The sidewalk seating area was wide enough to accommodate two rows of small tables. It was surrounded by a 3 foot high, gold canvas separating wall, which provided an entrance to the street.

Frankie's car and driver sat waiting a few car-lengths from the entrance to the outside dining. He knew that the restaurant was one of Bennie's favorites. It was partly because it was within walking distance to his home. Bennie liked to stay in his neighborhood.

Frankie opened his copy of the New York Post, ordered a glass of Chianti, and waited for Benny.

xxxxxxxxxx

Abby's phone rang early.

"Hello Abby. It's Hope. I trust I didn't wake you."

"No, I'm awake." She hoped that she didn't sound as sleepy as she felt.

"I haven't heard from you in a while. You've canceled the last couple of appointments. Is everything alright?"

"Yes. I've been very busy lately. Sorry. I'll call you next week to schedule something."

"I have a slot open today at 11:00. Why don't you come in then. You can tell me what's been going on with you."

I really don't want to see Hope right now, she thought, *just not in the mood.*

"Well, I don't know..."

"Great! I'll see you at 11, then."

"Okay." Abby hung up the phone and found her pillow again.

"Hi, Hope. Sorry, I'm a little late. My last meeting lasted a little longer than I thought."

"Not a problem, Abby. I didn't know you had another meeting this morning. I hope it was a successful one."

"Yes. Thanks." Abby knew she was a bad liar. So did Hope.

"Please come in and sit down."

"Thank you."

"So, what's new with you?"

"Nothing, really."

"How's your friend, Sarah?"

"She's not my friend. She's my intern."

"Oh, right. Sorry. How is she?"

"She's doing well. Thank you."

"I thought you might have brought her in, by now, to introduce me to her. I think I mentioned that I would like to meet her."

"Yes, you did mention that. But as I said, I don't think I can get her to come in here to see you." Abby, again, found herself getting aggravated in Hope's office.

"Yes, you did tell me that. However, I was hoping…"

"I'll ask again. Can we, please, talk about something else."

"Of course. What else would you like to talk about?"

"I don't know. Not that!"

"Okay. How's your job?"

"Good."

"Were you able to get that conservative endorsement?"

"Yes, I was. It wasn't cheap."

"I'm sorry?"

"Ya know, local politics. You gotta sell your soul."

"Yes. I guess that's true enough. I hope you didn't sell too much of it, though." Hope tried to give a look of reassurance.

"Just enough." Abby was looking at Hope now. She paused trying to formulate her next sentence.

"Something else on your mind, Abby?"

"Yes. I just learned that my father's death might not have been a suicide. Can you imagine after all these years?"

Hope reached for the box of tissues that she kept by her side. For a few moments the only sounds were that of Abby's soft weeping.

"I knew it. I just knew it. I knew he wouldn't do it. He loved me so much," she said in barely a whisper as she reached for another tissue.

Hope said nothing. She continued to lean in toward Abby, providing nonverbal support.

"Walter said that he learned from a good source that Jake Walsh might have done it."

"Jake Walsh? Where do I know that name from?"

"He was a big-time lawyer who got jammed up and went to prison. He's dead now. He was also Phillip's father."

"Your Phillip?"

"Yes. My Phillip."

"Wow! That's some connection. And now Phillip's dead too. Why would his father want to kill your dad?"

"Apparently my dad was scheduled to testify in the grand jury against Jake." The tears continued.

Hope looked away, not really knowing what to say. It was a place in which she was not accustomed to being.

"Well," she finally said, "this might help to alleviate some of your abandonment issues." She knew as soon as it came out her mouth that it was woefully inadequate for the moment. "Clinically speaking that is."

Abby, momentarily, looked up from her tissue. The sobbing continued. Hope decided it was best to let her cry for a bit.

"Thank goodness for Walter," Abby said, trying to regain her composure. "He's been a rock, my rock."

"Why do you say that?"

"He's been there through everything. He really cares; first man since my dad."

"Abby, sounds like you got a keeper."

"Yea. I think, maybe I do."

"Okay, when do you want to come in next week? And um, do you need a refill?"

xxxxxxxxxx

Frankie watched Benny as he approached the table. He didn't look up until Benny actually sat down.

"Hi, Benny. Thanks for meeting me here."

"No problem. What's up?"

"As I said on the phone I just wanted to make sure that we were good. The last meeting we had didn't end so well."

We're good as long as you keep earning. That's the way this game is played, Frankie. You know that."

Frankie smiled. "I'm well aware of how the game is played."

"Good. What are you gonna have." Benny looked down at his menu.

"Speaking of games, Benny. When are we going to get that money from your buddy? He's into me for 400 large."

"I know that. He's into me and three other members of my crew, also."

"That doesn't help me, Benny. I want my money. You vouched for this asshole; friend of yours, you said."

"You'll get your money..."

"When?"

"When I get it."

Frankie looked down at his paper. "Okay. I guess that will have to do."

"I'll have the rigatoni bolognese," Frankie said, looking up to the waiter.

"I'll have the same. Do you want a bottle of wine?"

"That's fine. Whatever you want."

"Okay. We'll take a bottle of Chianti, too. Your best one."

The waiter nodded. "Yes sir." He then retreated.

"Your pal needed the money for this revolutionary cleaning product. Needed 2 million to get this thing off the ground, right? Then the money was going to come rolling in, right? Well, is the product out there yet? Any purchase orders? Anything? Or just all bullshit?"

"It's almost certified by the CDC and the EPA. Just a few more steps he said."

"What the fuck? He couldn't get this going with 2 mil. Well,

I don't give a fuck. I want my money plus the vig we agreed on."

"Relax. I'll make a call after lunch."

Frankie changed the subject and it stayed changed for the duration of the lunch. Nothing more was said about the 400 large.

"I got it," Frankie said with a smile when the bill came.

"Thanks for lunch." Benny finished his last little bit of wine and put his napkin on the table.

"My pleasure."

"Do you have your car here?"

"Yes, it's right up the street. Why, you want to talk?"

"Yea, let's walk and talk for a few blocks."

"No problem. I'll have my driver follow us."

Benny nodded and got up from the table. Frankie put on his long black leather coat and followed him out to the sidewalk. The sun's warmth on this early spring day in Brooklyn was welcomed as the two men began to walk.

Frankie motioned to his driver to keep the big black SUV close to the two men as they walked side by side on the sidewalk. Frankie walked closest to the street.

They said nothing the first block or two. Frankie, knowing that they could no longer be seen by the side walk diners, spoke first. "What's on your mind, Benny?"

"Just want you to know that I don't need you to try and get tough with me. That's bullshit. You can't intimidate me, Pal. You'll get paid when I get paid and not a minute before. And you can tell anyone else that's bitchin' the same thing. They'll wait and they'll like it."

Frankie stopped and turned to Benny. Benny also stopped.

"Okay, Benny. That's fine. No hard feelings."

"No hard feelings as long as you know where you stand." Benny's hand met Frankie's extended hand and the understanding was confirmed.

While still holding Benny's right hand securely, Frankie produced a Glock 21, equipped with a silencer, from his left coat pocket. He very quickly placed the long black barrel tightly into Benny's gut and fired twice. The soft 'pop' sound that the pistol produced was barely above a whisper. Benny crumpled to the ground below his feet.

He moaned in agony and squirmed on the Brooklyn sidewalk, blood oozing from the wounds. Benny's fingers trying in vain to simultaneously stop the pain and the bleeding.

Frankie fired twice more into Benny's chest. The second shot rendered Benny motionless.

Frankie hurried to his waiting car and was blocks away before anyone noticed what had happened. Having breathed his last, Benny lay perfectly still with his eyes open, but they were blind to the commotion that began to take place above his motionless body.

Frankie's car pulled into a deserted lot not far from the Brooklyn Navy yard. Frankie got out of the car, lit a small, thin cigar and leaned against the side of his large black SUV.

He didn't have to wait long before a black 'S' class drove up and stopped a few imaginary parking spots away. A tall gray-haired man, wearing a long tan cashmere overcoat, stepped out of the backseat of the car.

Frankie did not wait to be summoned. He walked over to where the man stood, only a foot or two from his car.

"Hello, Frankie. Is he gone?"

"Yes, Neil. He's gone. Just like you said."

"Good. He got too careless. It's your crew now."

"Thank you."

"I had someone else take care of his buddy after he signed everything over to me."

"So then we'll all get our money."

"And then some."

"Thank you, Neil."

"And one more thing, your friend the judge, ya know the party girl. I might need her in about a month. She's on board right?"

"Yea, she's good. Just let me know what you need." Neil nodded once and got back in his car. Neil's limp was noticeable. Frankie knew how Neil got the limp but it didn't come to his mind very often any longer. It was part of who Neil was.

The car sped away leaving Frankie standing, watching. He waited a few minutes, maybe longer, before he returned to his car.

He needed to get to work now. He was the new Caperegime. It's a whole new ballgame now. As a 'Capo' he will be answering directly to an Underboss.

He wasn't worried. He got along well enough with Neil. But he could not ever get careless and he never would. Bennie was an asshole. "I'm no asshole," he said, aloud.

CHAPTER 11

Abby's thoughts were scattered since she spoke to Walter about her dad. Rarely did she focus on Phillip's murder, except to realize that a small caliber pistol was used on him as well. That was more than enough thought for Phillip.

Her mind flashed to a conversation that she had with

Sarah a few weeks ago. "Anything new, Sarah?"

"No, Judge. Not really."

"Okay now that we're out of the building you can call me Abby," the judge said with a smile as they walked out into the sidewalk.

Sarah smiled. "Okay."

"You want to stop by my place for a cocktail on your way home?"

"That sounds great, Abby. Listen, there is something that I think you should know."

"Let's wait until we get inside. Is Pinot Grigio good?" Abby asked as she removed her sweater.

"Yes, Abby. That'll be fine. Thanks."

Sarah sat at the island and watched Abby pour the wine. *Should I tell her what I heard?*

"Here you go." Abby placed a glass in front of Sarah on the granite counter-top and proposed a toast.

"To one of the few people in this world that I can trust. It's you and Walter, Sarah. There's no one else."

"Thank you, Abby." Sarah raised her glass in compliance, her mind still not completely in the moment.

"You said that you had something to tell me," Abby said, her first sip done.

"Yes." Sarah paused.

"Well?"

Sarah knew that if she paused much longer her loyalty would be questioned.

"Phillip was going to rat you out about the payoff. He didn't care who went down as long as you got hurt."

Abby couldn't help but smile. Her intern sounded more like a mobster than a law student. "I'm not surprised, but how do you know?"

"I overheard him talking to Lisa. As you know, Phillip was not big on discretion."

"Yes, I know."

"How did he know?"

"Don't know," she said.

Neither woman said anything for a few minutes.

Abby broke the silence. "Do you think he did?"

"Not sure but I was thinking the same thing."

"No, he couldn't have. I would have heard something by now." Abby paused. "But now, Lisa knows."

Sarah took another sip of wine and nodded. "That's right but you can trust her, right Abby?"

"I think so. She's been with me a long time. I can trust her." Her voice trailed off to a question. "I think I can trust her."

"Well, now there's three people in the world whose loyalty shouldn't be questioned, isn't there?" Sarah said, smiling, as she raised her glass to toast again.

xxxxxxxxx

Walter answered the door with the stem of a single red rose in his mouth. Abby giggled as he handed it to her.

"Thank you, Walter. You always make me smile."

"You've been making me smile since I first laid eyes on you at the Judges' Award Dinner. Thank you for coming into my life." Walter turned toward Abby.

Abby, still smiling, made herself comfortable in the sitting room.

"I made some eggplant dip for us to have with our wine. I hope you like it. I found it in an old cookbook I found lyin' around the house. And I picked up a nice bottle of Sancere for us to try."

"Thank you. The dip looks good; can't wait to try it." Walter sat down next to Abby with two half full glasses of wine. "Sorry I dropped the bomb on you the last time. I didn't mean to upset you. I just thought you should know."

"No worries, Walter. It didn't come as a complete surprise to me. I knew my father knew Jake. I just didn't know anything about the grand jury."

"Well, that changes things a bit. I mean the grand jury piece."

"Yes, it does. And, interestingly enough, Jake's relationship with my dad was a big reason for me picking Phillip to be my lawman."

"Really? So, you thought you could trust him because of that?"

"Yes. I guess I did."

Walter raised his eyebrows in response and looked away as his eyes followed his wine glass to his lips. Abby faced forward on the couch, not really looking at anything. Her sip of wine was long and deliberate.

"This dip is pretty good, isn't it?"

Abby just nodded in agreement; her eyes never changing their focus.

"Are you okay, Abby?"

"Yes, Walter. I'm okay." His question brought her back in the moment. It had its desired effect.

"You're sure?"

"Somehow, I thought having Phillip around would bring me closer to my dad. Ya know, kinda keep his memory alive."

Walter hugged Abby. "I guess I get that," he said.

xxxxxxxxxx

"So, you couldn't talk Walter into joining us today?" "No, I couldn't. Not today. Maybe next time."

Hope leaned back in her chair and put her pencil to her lips.

She paused before she spoke.

"You and Walter are becoming very close, aren't you?"

"Yes."

"Even intimate?"

"Yes. I guess that's right."

"And this is helping you get away from your 'inappropriate' behavior?"

"Yes." Abby was looking down now.

Hope paused, her eyes sympathetically watching Abby's every move. She leaned back with her notebook in hand still looking at Abby. Abby did not look up.

"But there is no Walter, is there, Abby? He's just in your head, isn't he? Someone that you can rely on. Someone who you can use to try to stop what you know is destructive behavior."

Abby didn't answer. She started to gently pull on the bottom edge of her sweater.

"Has Sarah met Walter?"

"No, not yet."

"Why not? Isn't she your friend and confident?"

"Yes, she is. The timing hasn't worked out. That's all. She knows all about him though, and he knows all about her."

"I think Walter comes from you, Abby." Hope paused for a reaction. "And I think we need to talk about that."

"Walter is real. He helps me. He listens to me. He loves me." Abby's words came slowly and quietly.

"Can you, please look at me for a moment, Abby?" Abby did, but only briefly. Before Hope continued she was focused on her sweater again.

"Can you describe Walter for me? What color hair does he have?"

"Salt and pepper."

"What about his height? Is he a tall man?"

"No, not too tall. I'm not doing this, Hope! Don't ask me any more question about Walter. He's real and he's helped me tremendously. I think I'm falling in love with him."

Hope sat up straighter. She said nothing. She just scribbled a note or two.

"That's enough for today. See you next week, Abby. I will see you next week, won't I?"

"Yes. I'll see you next week."

"Before you leave, do you need a refill?"

"No. Thanks."

xxxxxxxxxx

Abby didn't think that she would miss Phillip very much but she missed him even less than she thought. She barely thought about him. Phillip's replacement was a brilliant young woman.

Karen caught on very quickly and she was getting things done. The unsavory stacks of motions that dominated Phillip's office were, after only a couple of weeks, reduced by at least half.

An unintentionally attractive woman, she rarely looked away from her computer screen. She wore oval shaped rose-colored wire framed glasses and her dark brown hair was always tightly pulled back in a long pony tail.

"Judge, it's 9:15. Do want me to call up the reporter?" Lisa's question snapped Abby out of a trance. "Everything okay, Judge?"

"Yes, I'm fine Lisa. Please call the reporter."

"Okay, Judge," Lisa said, not at all satisfied with the judge's response. She looked back one last time as she left the room.

"All rise. The Honorable Justice Abigale Polk presiding." The clerk's powerful voice silenced the room full of whispering attorneys.

The judge took her seat on the bench. She was not going to stand today. "Please be seated. Call the first case, Mr. Clerk."

"Rosenburg vs J and P cleaning service."

"Plaintiff," a lawyer shouted.

"Defendant," another said, almost immediately following the first.

"Okay, gentlemen. Approach, please." She reviewed her notes on the file as the attorneys approached.

"Appearances, please, Counselors," requested the clerk with the thunderous voice.

"Just a minute, Gentlemen. Counselor, are you texting in my courtroom?" The judge was focused on a young lawyer in the first row.

"Yes, Judge. It was my office. Sorry."

"I don't care who it was. Don't you see all the signs posted in my courtroom? There is to be no cell phone use of any kind in my courtroom." The judge was standing now.

"I'm sorry, Your Honor. I was just confirming an appointment that I have this afternoon."

"I don't want to hear it. All these other lawyers have offices that they need to communicate with as well."

The judge turned to the court officer and said, "You will take this attorney into custody and charge him with contempt of court."

She sat down as the attorney was being handcuffed and brought to the holding cell in the back. "No cell phones in my court room," she muttered.

"And bring him back to me to be arraigned," the judge shouted as she shot up out of her chair.

"Yes, Judge," the court officer said, turning to face the judge. He led the young lawyer into the holding cell that flanked the courtroom.

A quiet murmur engulfed the courtroom and more than a few attorneys scurried out through the large door to the hallway with cell phones in hand.

The judge retired to her chambers leaving the lawyers who were arguing the motion at the bench looking at each other with files in hand. The clerk went about her business and the court reporter looked straight ahead, waiting.

xxxxxxxxxx

"Hope, I threw a lawyer in jail for an hour or two for texting in my courtroom," Abby offered before she sat down.

"We've talked about this behavior, Abby. Didn't we agree that it's a bit drastic?"

"I don't care. I'm the judge."

"Wouldn't a stern warning have sufficed?" A knock on the office door interrupted the conversation.

"Isn't this my time?" Abby was now lying down on the love seat, arms at her side, staring at the ceiling.

Hope opened the door. "Hi, my name is Walter. May I come in?"

"It's very nice to meet you, Walter," Hope said with a smile and an outreached hand.

"It's nice to meet you too, Hope."

"Won't you sit down and join us," Hope offered. Abby, sitting up now, silently, continued to fidget, on the love seat against the wall.

"It's gonna be okay, Honey." Walter said. He tried to comfort her by sitting next to her and calming her nervous hands in her lap with his.

Abby looked at him then quickly looked away. "Abby, do you want to say anything?"

Abby just shook her head in response to Hope's question.

"Can I say something, Hope?"

"Yes, of course… Well, I don't know Walter, maybe we should ask Abby. Is it all right if Walter tells us what's on his mind?" Abby nodded.

Hope looked at Walter. "What would you like to add?"

"I liked the relationship that Abby seemed to have with Sarah. She was a good friend to Abby. I thought she needed that in her life. I was happy for her."

"Did you ever meet Sarah?"

"No. The relationship that I described came entirely from my many conversations with Abby. I wanted to meet her but I never did."

"Why not?"

"I wasn't sure." Then he paused and looked at Abby. He held her hands a little tighter. "Until recently that is. Now, I don't think she exists."

"So, it's Sarah that you think doesn't exist. Can I ask what makes you think that?"

"A few pieces fell into place."

"Would you care to elaborate, Walter?"

Abby grabbed Walter's forearm and looked up at him, her eyes begging him to stop.

"It'll be okay, Abby," Walter whispered. "Hope needs to know. She can help." He leaned Abby's back against the back of the love seat.

"It was the picture," he said softly.

"What picture," Hope asked.

"She showed me an old picture of me, her, and her mom and dad. We were on a charter fishing boat. I was friendly with her dad from work. He kinda took me under his wing."

Walter stopped. His sympathetic gaze was lost on Abby. She was still, as if in a trance, staring straight ahead.

His mind raced back to that day in his house.

"I have a little surprise for you, honey," she said reaching into her pocketbook. "I found an old picture you might like to see. Wait till you see it." He remembered thinking how excited she was.

"Look, see. That's me. I couldn't have been more than 10 or 11 there. What are you about 25 there?"

"I'm about 23 there, I think, Abby. I was in the clerk's office about a year or so."

"Yea, we were going fishing. You remember that day. I do. My dad took me fishing a few times. I remember all of them." She thought about her dad for a moment.

"Look who else is with us, Sarah."

"That's not Sarah, Abby. That's your mom."

"No! That's not my mom!"

Walter said nothing.

She held the picture closer to her face. "Oh, yes. You're right that's my mom. I don't know what I was thinking. I didn't even know Sarah then." Abby's nervous laugh ended quickly.

All three sat silently for a time. Hope and Walter first looking at each other then watched Abby, hoping in vain for a reasonable explanation. Abby couldn't look at anyone at that moment.

Then, finally, Hope spoke, very quietly. "So, Abby, there is no Sarah? Is that right?"

Abby said nothing. Her trance seemed unbreakable. "Well, that's enough for today. Let's talk about this in more detail next time. Okay, Abby." Abby nodded.

"C'mon, honey. Let's go home." Walter helped Abby up and with his arm around her shoulder, escorted her to the door. Walter noticed the moist trail of a tear or two on her cheeks, but he didn't stop. He thought he needed to get her home.

No more talking today, not even an acknowledgement. Any further discussions would have to wait for another day. Today he was determined to keep things light. He had to, for Abby.

www.ingramcontent.com/pod-product-compliance
Lightning Source LLC
LaVergne TN
LVHW020440070526
838199LV00063B/4794